RUNNING WITH HORSES

A Story of Love and Murder

©2015 William H. Joiner, Jr.

All rights reserved. No part of this publication may be reproduced or used in any form or by any means, graphic, electronic or mechanical, including photocopying, recording, taping, or information and retrieval systems without written permission of the publisher.

Edited by Missy Brewer

Book design by Michael Campbell, MCWriting.com

Cover design by Bryan Gehrke, MyCoverDesigner.com

ISBN: 978-1517470838

For more information visit www.williamjoinerauthor.com

Buck leaned back in the booth at Fernando's Hideaway, slowly sipping on a cold longneck. He closed his eyes, savoring the taste of the beer. Buck snapped to attention when he heard the squeaky voice of Chopper Barker. "Well, well, well—what do we have here?"

The gravelly sound of Chopper's brother Babe declared, "Why, dear brother, I believe it's the famous Buck Morgan. Hey Buck, how's it hanging?"

Chopper commanded the patrons, the waitresses and the bartenders, "Everybody out! Everybody except our guest of honor, the great Buck Morgan." Every inhabitant of the bar scurried out without so much as a backward glance. It was common knowledge that when the Barker brothers were on the prod, the farther one could get away from them, the better. Chopper grinned sarcastically. "Your luck has finally run out, Morgan. You're about to find out what happens to them that crosses the Barker brothers."

Chopper confidently fingered his hand axe as Babe tapped the big end of his baseball bat on the palm of one hand. Buck slid out of the booth as he reached around to the small of his back and smoothly pulled his Smith & Wesson .38 Special from its holster.

Buck smirked at the gangsters as he cocked the pistol. "It's just like you two dickheads to bring an axe and a bat to a gun fight."

Babe snickered as he called back over his shoulder, "Boys!" Four more hoodlums quickly entered and spread out, each armed with a pistol or a rifle.

There was no fear in Buck's eyes, even though he was outgunned four to one and outmanned six to one. Buck said, "Well, boys, it appears we have us a Mexican standoff."

Chopper sneered, "We ain't got no Messican standoff! If you ain't noticed, I'm no pepper belly! If you hadn't pulled that damn gun, we was gonna cut and whomp you to death. Now, we're just gonna shoot the shit out of ya!" Chopper paused to give Buck a chance let it sink in what was about to happen.

When Chopper felt the time was right, he shrilly ordered his men, "Kill him!" The guns all banged at once and gun smoke clouded the air. The bullets zinged towards Buck like a swarm of deadly hornets.

RUNNING *with* HORSES

A STORY OF LOVE AND MURDER

WILLIAM H. JOINER, JR.

CONTENTS

Obadiah and Ruth *1*

The Mothers *7*

Leonard Culpepper *9*

In the Cards *13*

Off to the Races *15*

The Auditor *17*

Buttermilk *21*

The Joy of Carol *23*

New Life *29*

Cowboy *31*

The First Ride *33*

Little Timmy *37*

Giving the Finger *41*

The First Race *45*

The Masterson Game *51*

Twins *57*

The Record Run *59*

The Text Message *65*

The Vegas Remedy *69*

Fernando's Hideaway *73*

Closing The Mouth *79*

The Revival *85*

The Kentucky Derby *91*

Wins and Losses *101*

Adalwolf Dittmar *103*

Monaco *109*

The Clean Break *123*

Horse Trading *127*

Julie Strong *131*

Celebrities *139*

The Calling *141*

Fight for Her *145*

Acknowledgements *149*

OBADIAH AND RUTH

BUCKMINSTER MORGAN was the only child of Obadiah and Ruth Morgan. Obadiah named his son Buckminster after hearing about a grand church in England, Buckminster Abbey. Obadiah hoped that God would be so pleased with his choice of names for his son, God would surely give Obadiah a mega-church in Texas to pastor. Obadiah would close his eyes and picture the massive stained-glass windows of his new church.

Obadiah was certain that he was going to become the next great TV evangelist, although he definitely had a face for radio. Obadiah was 5 feet 6 inches tall and weighed 130 pounds soaking wet. His muddy brown eyes were too close together. His nose resembled the beak of a bird and his chin came to a point. Despite his unimpressive physical appearance, most people were afraid of him. When he was mad, which was most of the time, a dark scowl came over his face. That, coupled with a slightly unhinged look in his eyes, would cause an observer's skin to crawl.

Obadiah answered what the thought was God's call on his life by preaching on street corners. His intentions initially might have been good, but the good was far outweighed by the bad as Obadiah called down the fires of Hell on all the sinners within the sound of his voice. Only those who were gluttons for punishment stayed for his full sermons.

Once, while Obadiah was thrashing about in righteous indignation, he was interrupted by an onlooker. "Hey mister, do you work for the post office?"

Obadiah was puzzled, "No! Why do you ask, sinner?"

The man walked off saying to another gawker, "Whew, that's a relief! I was scared that ol' boy was about to go postal!"

Obadiah yelled after him, "Repent, sinner! Repent, you nest of vipers! The judgment of Almighty God is at hand! You are going to burn in hell!"

Ruth Morgan mostly went unnoticed due to her mousy appearance. She tended to blend into the background. Ruth was a small woman with prematurely gray hair and gray eyes. Even the pallor of her skin was gray. Adding to her mouse impression was a thin pair of lips that constantly pursed and unpursed, revealing two small buck teeth. Ruth completed her rodent image by nibbling at her food when she ate.

The Morgans lived in a low-end trailer park in a little 8-by-34 foot trailer. The fifteen-lot park was littered with old cars up on blocks, discarded washing machines, and trash in general. The Morgans and their neighbors were classic examples of "white trash."

The Morgans' standard of living fell below the poverty line. Obadiah earned an average of about two dollars a day preaching his version of the Gospel. If he had gotten paid per the volume of his voice instead of the content of his message, the Morgans would have been a wealthy family. The family's main income came from Ruth's meager paycheck as an aide at a local nursing home.

The Morgans qualified for all the government subsidies from free cheese to food stamps. The subsidies were originally designed for those who had temporarily fallen on hard times. Some families, like the Morgans, felt like the subsidies were a permanent entitlement. In some twisted way, Obadiah counted the freebies as his contribution to the family's budget, although he never went to the government offices to collect the welfare. Instead, Obadiah insisted, "Woman, you go pick up our bounty. It's just not fitting for me to be involved in such a demeaning type of transaction. God wouldn't want His Called to be sullied by undignified tasks."

When Buck was born, he was a strapping, robust boy, weighing in at almost eleven pounds. He had a full head of blond hair and sparkling blue eyes. It was a tie among who was the most shocked at Buck's appearance: Obadiah, Ruth, the doctor, the nurses or anybody else who compared him to his parents. It was as if aliens had brought the Morgans a baby from a far-off planet.

Buckminster Morgan got very little teasing about his first name for two reasons. One, he went by the name of Buck. Two, Buck's presence was intimidating even as a small boy. Buck's good friends could tease him, but acquaintances never considered it. Buck's natural demeanor, which included a stare that some likened to a Mafia hit man, was such that most would judge it tantamount to pulling the whiskers of a lion. Common sense dictated that it was not a good idea.

Buck could lose his intense persona and flash a brilliant smile, which transformed his face into one of warmth and charm. This was not contrived. The equal ability to repel and attract was who Buck was. Which side of him was displayed depended on whether he liked someone or not. Another factor was whether there was an attractive woman involved. Buck was never duplicitous. He expressed what he thought.

Buck grew up to be 6 feet 4 inches and 220 pounds of packed muscle. He had the body of a natural athlete. When you added in his blond hair and piercing blue eyes, he attracted females like bees to honey.

All through middle and high school, Buck was the star athlete on the football, basketball and baseball teams. He was the quarterback on the football team, the point guard on the basketball team and a dominating pitcher on the baseball team. Starting in his sophomore year in high school, Buck began receiving scholarship offers to play ball in college. The offers ranged from private schools like TCU, SMU and Baylor to the large public schools, University of Texas in Austin and University of Oklahoma in Norman. Buck could have gotten a free education at any university in the country. Knowing his abilities, SMU even said he could play on their football, basketball and baseball teams.

Buck confounded everyone when he announced the week before his high school graduation that he wasn't going to college. His father, Obadiah, was especially chagrinned as most of the colleges either hinted at or told him in no uncertain terms that if Buck signed with their school, there would be a big, although illegal, "signing bonus" paid to Obadiah.

Obadiah was furious. "Boy, I have fed you, clothed you and given you a roof over your head, and this is the way you repay me. God will smite you for this!"

From an early age, Buck had known what kind of man his father was. At twelve years of age, Buck supported himself financially by taking a part-time job in addition to attending school and participating in sports. Buck grinned. "Sorry, Dad. I guess you'll just have to keep hitting the street corners."

When Buck was a young boy, Obadiah would beat him with a two-feet-long 2x4 at any imagined violation of Obadiah's rules. "God told me, 'spare the rod and spoil the child!' I'm doing this for your own good!"

The beatings stopped when Buck was ten years old. He had grown big enough and strong enough that he ripped the board from his father's hand as Obadiah started another "discipline" session. Buck waved the 2x4 under his father's nose. "If you ever put your hands on me again, I will beat you with your own board." Obadiah blanched as he slunk away, muttering about how sharper than a serpent's tooth is an ungrateful child.

While Buck had more tender feelings for his mother because he counted her as a victim too, he harbored resentment that she had let Obadiah abuse him when he was too young and small to defend himself. His sophomore year, Buck had saved enough money to rent an apartment. He was glad to leave the little 8-by-34-foot trailer where they lived. When Buck moved out on his own, he had very little contact with his parents after that.

At his last visit with them, Buck tried to make conversation, "Dad, how is the preaching going? Are you getting very much in donations?" Obadiah replied with a shrug of his shoulders, "Okay."

Buck tried his mother, "Mom, how's your job at the nursing home?" Ruth mimicked her husband, "Okay."

After sitting there though fifteen minutes of silence, Buck gave up and left.

Regardless of how neglectful his parents were, it still hurts Buck's feelings when he finally came to terms that they cared little, if any, about him.

Not long after he got out of high school, Buck read a small article on the third page of the *Dallas Morning News*. It said that Obadiah and Ruth Morgan were gunshot victims in what appeared to be a murder/suicide. The paper didn't say which one was the shooter. Buck thought it might be either one of them: Obadiah in a self-righteous fit of rage or Ruth pushed past her breaking point.

Buck did locate and visit their graves one time. It was a gray, overcast day that perfectly represented the misspent life of Obadiah and Ruth Morgan. He brought flowers, but was puzzled that he could not muster any tears. Buck never went back.

THE MOTHERS

Buck was a favorite with girls and women. His looks and personality gave the opposite sex a case of loose panties. It climaxed his senior year with a hair-pulling, name-calling fight in the hallway between Beth Holloway, the head cheerleader, and Ann Atkins, the star player on the girls' basketball team.

Ann pulled Beth to the floor with her fingers entwined in Beth's long blonde hair. Ann screamed, "Stay away from him, bitch!"

Beth rolled on the floor, kicking at Ann, trying to grab Ann's short black hair as she squealed, "He doesn't love you, slut! Buck loves me!" It took the principal and four teachers to separate the girls.

There was also major tension and animosity between Beth's mother and Ann's mother. Most thought it was because of the fight between their daughters. A few suspected, correctly, that their dislike for each other was mostly generated by their own romantic interests in Buck. It was rumored that he had dalliances with both women. Both women were part of the boob-job-and-cocaine mind set. That left a lot of leeway for one's moral compass. Buck never said he had sex with the two women, but he never denied it either.

Beth's mother, Caroline, and Ann's mother, Marcella, accidentally bumped into each other in the restroom at a local restaurant.

As they stared daggers, Caroline said contemptuously, "I hear you're as big a whore as your little slutty daughter!"

Marcella retorted, "Have you screwed all the players on the football team? Your bitch of a daughter has!" The encounter didn't come to blows, but several women were occupying the stalls and overheard the exchange. Pretty soon everyone in their part of town heard about the confrontation.

LEONARD CULPEPPER

Buck was easily the most popular boy in school, admired and respected by students and teachers alike. Leonard Culpepper was easily the least popular boy in school. Leonard was the classic nerd, complete with a pocket protector and thick, black-framed glasses held together by tape on the nose bar.

Leonard was skinny and frail, and was an easy target of the school bullies. Billy Bob Thornton, who was a hulking defensive tackle on the football team, loved to say, "I don't believe ol' Leonard could whip the gnats off his own ass."

One day Buck noticed a commotion down the hall. When he went to investigate, he found Billy Bob and some of the other football players had surrounded Leonard and were pushing him back and forth between them as a crowd of kids snickered and laughed. Leonard's glasses and all the pens in his pocket protector were scattered along the floor of the hall.

Billy Bob taunted, "Come on, Leonard. You don't have to take this shit! I'll tell you what. I'll give you the first punch. Go ahead. Knock me on my ass!" Billy Bob stuck his tongue in the side of his cheek causing his cheek to bulge out, creating a target for Leonard.

When Buck looked at Billy Bob tormenting Leonard, he didn't see Billy Bob's face. He saw his father's face. His anger welled up in him for all those years when he was bullied by his father. For his entire life, Buck would always hate a bully.

No one noticed Buck until he stepped through the gang of kids and punched Billy Bob square on the jaw. The blow caused Billy Bob's head to snap back and he landed flat on his back, unconscious. All the kids were shocked. Some because they couldn't believe someone had cold-cocked a beast like Billy Bob. Some because someone like Buck would take up for someone like Leonard.

Buck ordered the football players, "Pick up Leonard's stuff and put it back exactly like you found it!" As they scurried around replacing Leonard's belongings, Buck announced, "Tell everybody in this damn school that Leonard is my best friend. If you screw with Leonard, you screw with me!"

Buck put his arm around Leonard's shoulders. "Why don't you and me go to the Dairy Queen? The ice cream is on me."

Leonard smiled gratefully as he looked up to Buck. "Thanks, Buck. I would like that."

The next day Buck didn't wait for Billy Bob to find him. Buck went looking for him. Buck found him in the weight room. Buck coldly stared at Billy Bob. "Hey, I just wanted to check to see if you got anything to say to me?" Most bullies are cowards at heart. Billy Bob was no exception as he muttered, "I guess not, but don't you ever hit me again."

Buck threatened, "Don't start any shit with Leonard and there won't be any shit with me."

It took a few days for Leonard to realize that his status at school was now completely different than it once was. He noticed that he was getting respect from the other kids. An even bigger surprise was when he saw fear in some of their eyes. Leonard actually started to get a little cocky.

Once, two linebackers were roughhousing each other in the hall and one accidentally bumped into Leonard. The 130-pound Leonard scowled at the 220-pound football player, "Watch where you're going. You guys are not the only people in this hall!"

The linebacker patted Leonard on the shoulder. "You're right, man. Sorry!"

Leonard smiled as he thought to himself, *All right! I've got my shit together!* Buck had changed his life.

IN THE CARDS

Buck needed more money than his part-time job provided. He had become a fan of Texas Hold 'Em by watching the poker tournaments on TV. Buck bought Doyle Brunson's book *Super System* and wore the thick book out by reading it from cover to cover until it became tattered.

Buck looked for local games to play in. At first it was with other students, but quickly graduated to card games with grown men. He was a natural. Buck had a sixth sense when it came to poker. The truth was he would rather play cards than football, basketball or baseball.

There was a weekly Hold 'Em tournament on Monday nights at the Meadowbrook Country Club. Buck was working there as a part-time greenskeeper. All the local businessmen who played golf knew Buck from the Friday night high school football games. Even though they were grown men and he was a high school boy, they hero-worshipped the All State quarterback.

Buck overheard a group of men discussing the poker game which was to be played that night. He asked Herb Street, who owned the local hardware store, "Excuse me, Mr. Street. Can anyone play in the poker game? What's the buy-in?"

Herb said, "Anyone can play who has the $100 buy-in." Buck didn't have $100. He tried to conceal his disappointment, but it showed on his face. "Thanks, Mr. Street. I'll keep that in mind."

As he was leaving the club, Herb went up to Buck and put a piece of paper in Buck's front pocket. He whispered, "Come play cards with us tonight, boy. Only, I hope you're not as good a card player as you are a quarterback." Herb slapped Buck on the back, laughed and walked off.

After work, Buck checked the piece of paper. It was a crisp, new hundred dollar bill, folded in quarters. Buck played in the game that night. He left a $900 winner. In private, Buck tried to give Herb his $100 back, but Herb refused. "Nope, it's been worth that hundred for the entertainment of watching you play ball. One thing, don't tell anybody about the money! It might get you ruled ineligible to play ball. People would have my ass if they knew I was the reason you couldn't play ball."

The next day, one of the other men who played in the card game came by the hardware store. When he saw Herb, he said, "That damn kid sure got lucky last night!"

Herb responded, "Lucky, my ass! He beat the hell out of us 'cause he was better than us."

The man continued, "If that's true, how'd he get so good?"

Herb snorted, "How'd he get good enough to be an All State quarterback? He just is."

After graduating from high school, Buck decided to become a professional poker player. He became a regular among the Dallas poker games. Because of his age, Buck was welcomed by the city players. They thought this young, wet-behind-the-ears kid would be easy pickings. They were wrong. Buck walked away a winner in most of the games he played in.

OFF TO THE RACES

While he was good at it, the grind and tedium of daily poker games got on his nerves. Buck loved the outdoors and being in the sunshine. He longed for a respite from the indoor poker rooms.

Buck was attracted to horse racing and wanted to try his hand at it. He had no interest in buying a horse, entrusting it to a trainer and becoming a spectator. After spending a great amount of time at the training barns of racetracks, befriending top trainers and watching their training methods, Buck was confident he could be a successful trainer.

After watching the bullshit that trainers who trained for the public had to endure, Buck had no desire to put up with owners who could be overbearing and have unrealistic expectations. Successful people from other businesses who bought race horses just assumed that because they owned the horse, it was guaranteed to be a success. The condition is known as "barn blindness." If the horse is in their barn, it must be a success. If it wasn't, it had to be the dumb-ass trainer's fault.

Buck had enough money saved from playing poker that he could get in the racing game if he started modestly. Part of Buck's success playing cards was his friendship with Wendell "Ace" Wiggins. During the first time where both Buck and Ace were playing at the same table, Ace tipped back his cowboy hat, chewed on his cigar, grinned and winked at Buck. "Boy, I believe you got a little rattlesnake in you."

This began a friendship that turned into Ace becoming Buck's closest friend and mentor even though there was a forty year difference in their ages. Ace's advice about how to play people and not their cards was invaluable in developing Buck into a first-class poker player. As a coach, Ace knew when to praise and when to admonish. "Boy, the way you played that hand when you had pocket kings was about the dumbest thing I've ever seen!"

THE AUDITOR

B
uck had been on his own for a number of years. He had to adjust at a young age, when he was still just a boy, to being a man. Buck had to assume all the adult responsibilities including filing tax returns.

Buck had been filing his own tax returns for years. Whenever a taxpayer lists his occupation as a professional gambler, his returns are going to be more closely examined than the average Joe. One day Buck received an official letter from the IRS. Buck knew it was official because it was addressed to Buckminster Morgan. Buck swallowed hard when he read that he was being audited.

Buck told Ace, "I'm not going to lie, the IRS scares me a little."

Ace retorted, "You should be scared of them. They won't throw you in jail. They'll throw you so far under the jail they'll have to shoot beans to you with a rifle to feed you."

Buck frowned. "Thanks for all the comfort!"

Ace muttered, "I ain't your momma."

The day Buck dreaded finally came, the day when he was supposed to meet with an IRS agent. The Internal Revenue Service occupied an imposing building on Gessner Road in Houston. Buck was summoned for the meeting at 8:00am and instructed to bring all his records.

When Buck checked in at the front desk, the receptionist said, "Ms. Strickland will be with you in a minute. I will let her know that you're here." Buck was relieved when he learned that the IRS agent was a woman. He thought he could use the same charm on her that he used to charm the pants off most women.

The receptionist said, "Ms. Strickland can see you now. Take the hallway to the right to Room 104." Buck's confidence drained away when he stepped through the doorway to meet Ms. Strickland.

Gladys Strickland, a prim, grim-faced woman with her hair pulled into such a tight bun that it appeared to be painful, looked over her horn-rimmed glasses. "Sit down, Mr. Morgan. I assume you brought all your records as instructed."

Buck stuck out his hand in greeting. When Gladys just looked at it, Buck awkwardly pulled it back. Buck put on his most dazzling smile and cheerfully said, "Miss Strickland, I am glad to meet you."

Gladys corrected him, "It's not Miss or Mrs., it's Ms. This is not a social meeting, Mr. Morgan. It is a business meeting. We, here at the IRS, conduct our business in a serious manner. I suggest you do likewise."

Buck though, *Oh, hell. This barracuda is going to try to send me up the river. I wonder if I can outrun her?*

Buck dumped out his sack of bank statements on her desk. Gladys asked, "Is this all?"

Buck was starting to get irritated. "What else do you want? Those are my damn bank statements!"

Gladys snapped, "Mr. Morgan, you need to watch your language or I will call security."

Buck made a visible effort to calm down. "Okay, Ms. Strickland, I apologize. What other kind of records do you want?"

Gladys's voice did the impossible: it became even more strident. "Mr. Morgan, let's don't play games. We, here at the IRS, know that professional gamblers hide a lot of their income because you deal in cash. How much income are you hiding, Mr. Morgan?"

Buck had enough. "Ms. Strickland, I don't think you and I are going to get along. I want to see your supervisor."

Gladys responded, "That would be a waste of time, Mr. Morgan. We, here at the IRS, have all received the same training. It won't make any difference whom you speak with."

Buck insisted, "Your supervisor, Ms. Strickland!"

Gladys dialed her phone. "Sir, my eight o'clock, Buckminster Morgan, wants to meet with you… Yes, sir… Very good, sir." Gladys announced, "My supervisor will be right down."

They sat in silence until Buck asked, "Sooo, I guess you and I getting together after work tonight for a few drinks and some laughs, is out of the question?" Gladys just glared at him.

Shortly, a trim athletic man came through the door. "Mr. Morgan, please gather your records and follow me to my office." As Buck trailed the IRS agent down the hall to his office, he couldn't shake the feeling that they had met before. When they entered the agent's office, he said, "Please shut the door behind you."

When Buck shut the door and turned around, the IRS supervisor grinned, grabbed Buck's hand and began pumping it vigorously. "Hey Buck, how've you been?"

It dawned on Buck why this guy was so familiar. "Leonard… Leonard Culpepper, is that you?"

Leonard laughed, "Yeah, it's me all right!"

Buck stammered, "B… bu… but, you look so different!"

Leonard laughed again. "Well, Buck, it's been what… five years? A lot can change in five years. After I graduated from high school, I became a physical fitness nut! I lift regularly and run a few marathons every year."

Buck was still stunned, "You've done a hell of a job, old friend. Congratulations."

Leonard replied, "Actually, Buck, I owe it all to you. You gave me the confidence I needed in high school. Without your help, I would have been afraid to even try. I don't know that I ever thanked you properly for what you did for the class nerd. Thank you from the bottom of my heart!"

Buck was embarrassed. "Hell, I didn't do all that much. You did the work. I'm proud of you, Leonard." Buck set his sack of bank statements of Leonard's desk.

Leonard interjected, "Oh yes, we need to continue the audit." As Buck looked on nervously, Leonard opened the sack. He didn't take out the bank statements, just looked in the sack. Leonard closed it up, "Looks like everything is in order here. The audit is complete."

Buck exclaimed, "That's it?" Leonard grinned as he mocked Gladys, "We, here at the IRS, don't like the taxpayers to argue with us. The audit is over. You passed with flying colors."

Buck fist-bumped Leonard. "Thanks, brother. I owe you big-time!"

Leonard shook his head. "You don't owe me a damn thing."

Buck passed Gladys in the hall on his way out. He tried to put a worried scowl on his face befitting someone who just had his ass chewed out by IRS Chief Examiner Culpepper.

BUTTERMILK

///////////////////

Buck bought his first yearling at the Fasig-Tipton Yearling Sale that summer in Houston. In analyzing the yearlings offered for bid before the sale, a cream colored colt with an ink-black mane and tail from nondescript breeding caught Buck's eye. He liked the way the colt was put together. The colt had balanced confirmation from the angle of his neck tying into his shoulders to the angle of his shoulder to his strong hamstrings. The colt had good knees, perfect feet and was completely straight when he walked. Buck also noticed his oversized nostrils, which would supply additional oxygen to his bloodstream, giving him an advantage when he ran.

Because the colt's breeding was pedestrian, Buck knew the price would not be ridiculously high. The colt had enough minor stakes winners in his pedigree to qualify him for the select sale, but not much else was impressive in his lineage.

All that being said, Buck knew that there was a major factor which could not be measured: the horse's heart. Would the colt be a competitor? Buck had a feel for animals, and horses in particular. When he looked the colt in the eye, Buck felt like there was a spark there that could be a link to how big a heart this colt had.

When the bidding was over, Buck was able to buy the colt for $15,000.00. When Ace joined him at the back stalls in the sale barn to look over his new horse, Buck asked, "What do you think

I should name him?" Ace thought for a minute before saying, "His name is Buttermilk. He's the same color as the buttermilk I used to drink as a kid."

Buck sputtered, "Ace, that's got to be the dumbest name I've ever heard for a race horse! His name should be something regal and make you think of how fast he is."

Ace responded, "Well, I'll tell you, sonny boy, them big ol' glasses of buttermilk used to go through me like shit through a goose. Now, that is pretty damn fast!"

Buck acknowledged the colt's distant ancestor, the great Bold Ruler, by registering the colt's name as Bold Buttermilk. Normally, a horse owner will check with the Jockey Club registry to make sure a proposed name had not been previously used. Buck didn't bother. He was sure nobody else had ever been fool enough to name their horse Bold Buttermilk. He was right.

THE JOY OF CAROL

It was during that sale Buck met Carol Martin at the end of the day at the after-hours bar sponsored by Fasig-Tipton. Carol was a tall, willowy brunette with a runway model's good looks. She worked in public relations for a Houston bank.

Buck introduced himself, giving her his most charming smile. "Hi, I'm Buck Morgan. Now—don't tell me. I know I've seen you in the movies. You were in… it's right on the tip of my tongue… I don't know why I can't think of the name of that dang movie, but you are my favorite actress!"

Carol giggled as she extended her hand. Buck squeezed her hand more than he shook it, maybe just a little too long. Carol flashed her own dazzling smile. "Mr. Morgan, may I ask you a question?"

Buck still held her hand. "Absolutely, and please, call me Buck."

Carol replied, "Great! Buck, here's what I want to know. Are you always full of shit or are you making a special effort just for me?" A surprised Buck first sputtered, then doubled over with laughter. Carol joined him, breaking up in merriment.

Buck composed himself, finally using a napkin from the table to wipe away his tears from laughing so hard. Buck grinned. "Okay, you got me, but you *are* beautiful. The only reason you're not in the movies is the morons out in Hollywood don't know who you are. Seriously, I want to know you. What's your name?"

Carol thought to herself, *I've just met this guy and I think I'm already falling for him. He's just so damn good looking and funny too. I need to be careful before I end up doing something I regret.* Carol coolly said, "I'm Carol Martin. I'm not an actress. I work for Houston National Bank—not quite as glamorous as being an actress."

The next thing they knew, four hours had passed. Buck and Carol realized it was getting late when they noticed the wait staff were folding tablecloths and putting everything away.

Buck said, "Carol, I can't remember when I've had this much fun. Would you like to go somewhere else and continue the evening?"

Carol thought for a minute before deliberately applying the brakes to her runaway emotions. "I think we need to call it a night, but there's a polo match at the Houston Polo Club tomorrow. Would you like to go?"

The next day dawned bright and sunny. There were a few cotton clouds whose only purpose was to highlight the deep blue of the sky. The temperature was a mild 75 degrees. All in all, a perfect day for being outdoors.

When Buck met Carol at the polo grounds, she was wearing a bright yellow sun dress with a matching wide-brimmed hat. They watched the game as they talked. Buck admired the horses, but his attention kept going back to Carol's face. He wasn't sure that he had ever known anyone whose face reflected joy the way Carol's did.

At the halftime of the match, fans traditionally went on the field to smooth out the ground torn up by the horses' hooves. The sexual tension that was between them the night before carried over to today and was now off the charts. Instead of groundskeeping, Buck and Carol used that time to take a walk into the thick woods adjacent to the field.

Once they were safely out of sight and hearing, Buck picked out a tree with a horizontal limb that was about butt-high to Carol. As he kissed Carol, he backed her up to the limb. Their passions flared when their bodies pressed against each other. Carol relaxed and leaned back on the limb, allowing it to support her. Their kisses became more passionate and Buck's hands were eagerly exploring her body. Carol gasped as she grabbed Buck's hand. "Stop!"

A disappointed Buck thought they were going back to the polo match. Carol surprised him as she quickly shimmied out of her panties and shoved them in her purse.

After Buck hiked up her dress, they took their time enjoying the delicious pleasures of each other's bodies. Buck finished with a flourish, sending them both into euphoria. After they had adjusted their clothes, Carol suggested, "I imagine the polo match is over. Would you like to go back to my apartment?" Buck was more than agreeable as he noticed that Carol never put her panties back on.

They spent the next two days in each other's arms, interrupted only by sleep and sending out for the occasional pizza, with one major exception. The first night, Buck woke up as he heard a prowler in the kitchen. He slipped on his boxers and grabbed a large figurine of a cat that was on Carol's dresser. Armed with the statue, Buck stepped around the corner of the hall into the kitchen to confront the intruder.

Buck was stunned! It was Carol, fully clothed, munching on a piece of leftover pepperoni. He stammered, "But... but... how did you get dressed so fast?"

She laughed, "I guess you mean Carol. I'm her twin sister, Cheryl." Cheryl held out her hand. As Buck shook it, he exclaimed, "I'm Buck. Hell, I haven't even figured out your sister yet! Now, I've got another one to try to make some sense of."

Cheryl giggled, eerily sounding like Carol. "Well, Buck, it's nice to meet you, but it's late. I'm going to bed." As she headed for her bedroom, Cheryl turned and said, "Buck, my sister is the nicest person in the world. If she likes you, I like you. But, let me give you fair warning. If you hurt her, I will hurt you. I promise you won't want to tell your friends that a 130-pound girl whipped your ass."

As Cheryl smiled sweetly, Buck grinned. "Yes, ma'am!"

Buck pulled off his boxers and crawled back into bed, cuddled up to Carol's back and draping his arm over her. When he softly chuckled, Carol sleepily said, "What's so funny?"

Buck replied, "I just wondered whose naked butt I was snuggled up against."

Carol laughed as she turned over to face him. "I'm going to guess you met my sister."

Buck kissed her. "Yeah, I met her and she scared the shit out of me, not once but twice. The first time I thought she might be a burglar and I was going to knock him out with your cat. The second time she threatened to beat my ass if I wasn't nice to you."

Carol joked, "You better listen to her. She's a badass."

Buck snickered, "Well, in that case, I better get back to being nice to you again. What's the tally now, five or six times?"

Carol moaned as she pressed up against him. "Who cares, as long as you're on your best behavior."

The next morning, Buck, Carol and Cheryl had breakfast together. As the girls cooked sausage and eggs, Buck asked, "Is there anything else about you girls I need to know?"

Carol replied, "Well, I told you I work for Houston National Bank, which is true, but I left out that my father is president of the bank, not that that's a big deal."

Cheryl added, "There's one other thing you need to know. You can forget about any ideas you might have of sleeping with both of us. That's not gonna happen!"

Carol shrieked, "Cheryl!"

Cheryl responded, "Well, it's true! Men are pigs. You need to always keep that in mind."

Good naturedly, Buck put his hands up in a defensive pose and asked, "Okay, sister Cheryl, what's your deal? Do you have a job or does some sugar daddy handle your expenses?"

Cheryl retorted, "I pay my own way, jackass. I am a commercial artist."

As Cheryl handed Buck her business card, Carol added, "And… she is crazy good!"

Buck read the card that said Cheryl specialized in painting portraits from photographs. Carol continued to brag on her sister. "When she's not painting, she volunteers for half a dozen children's charities. No one has a bigger heart than Cheryl!"

Buck replied, "Very impressive! I had no idea that I was dating Mother Theresa's sister!" Cheryl rolled her eyes and made a gagging noise.

NEW LIFE

The next day, Buck and Carol went with Cheryl to New Life, a home for abused wives and children. The director of New Life was Irma Washington, a stocky black woman with a master's degree in psychology. Irma greeted Cheryl by throwing her arms around Cheryl and hugging her tightly to her ample bosom, "There's my girl! God, I love this woman! I'd hate to have to run this place without her!"

Cheryl's muffled voice could barely be heard. "Irma, you're killing me. I can't breathe. Let me up." Irma roared boisterously and pulled Cheryl out of her mammary canyon. Cheryl gasped for air as Carol laughed hysterically, tears pouring down her cheeks.

Irma turned her attention to Buck. "And who does this young man belong to, Cheryl or Carol?" Buck made a show of taking an exaggerated deep breath, holding his nose, preparing for the breasts of death. Irma cackled loudly as she hugged Buck's neck, "This boy is all right. He's gonna fit right in here!"

The girls took the time to visit the women and children who were living there, finding out what each woman and each child needed. They made sure every woman and child's needs were met.

While they were doing that, Irma filled in Buck. "Let me tell you something, young man, about what kind of women you're involved with." Irma got serious, looking Buck squarely in the eye. "God never made any better girls than these two. Anything that needs done around here, they do it. Cheryl auctions off her art work to benefit New Life. Carol has us hooked up with Houston National Bank. If we didn't get the funding from the bank every month, we'd have to close our doors."

Irma paused to wipe tears from her eyes, "Many women and children owe their lives to the work here at New Life. We help them escape a life of abuse and get a fresh start. Carol and Cheryl Martin are absolutely essential to our facility. You better have the best of intentions for Carol. If I hear of you hurting her, I will hunt you down like a dog."

Buck smiled. "What is it about me that makes people want to put me on notice that I better be on my best behavior with Carol?" Buck's smile widened into a grin. "If I said so much as a cross word to her, I think a posse would form carrying tar and feathers!"

Irma hugged him and laughed, "And don't you forget it, mister."

On the way back to the apartment, Buck said, "Ladies, I am more than impressed. You guys are rock stars as far as I'm concerned. Whatever you need me to do at New Life, I'm in."

Carol snuggled up to Buck. "Thanks, honey."

Cheryl joked, "You may not be such an asshole after all!"

Buck replied, "Give it up, Cheryl. The jig is up. You've been busted. The tough guy act won't wash anymore. I've seen who you really are. I'm proud to call you my friend."

As Carol and Cheryl both teared up, Cheryl meekly said, "Shut up."

COWBOY

Buck had had a steady girlfriend only a couple of times in his life. He was now 24 and didn't live life as recklessly and as wide open as he did in his late teens and early twenties. Buck had lost count of his number of sexual encounters. The vast majority were one night stands. There were a couple of women he saw more than once, but not many.

Buck had just turned 20 when he was approached one night in a country and western bar. Through the cigarette smoke and the neon lights, the blue-eyed honey blonde smiled and said, "Howdy, cowboy. I got a little problem, but I'm thinking you can solve it for me."

Buck nodded his head, "Little lady, I'm sure I can solve all your problems. What do you need?"

The blonde answered, "Well, my name is Donna and my roommate just broke up with her boyfriend and she's really sad. I'm thinking a big dose of you might cheer her right up."

Buck grinned. "Where is your friend?" Donna pointed to a table across the dance floor where a short brunette waved with just her fingers when she saw Buck look at her.

Buck stroked his chin as if he was contemplating whether he was going to leave with the girls or not. Of course, he had already decided he was going when he checked the girls out. Both wore short shorts exposing the bottoms of their butt cheeks and tank tops revealing they didn't believe in bras. Buck was guessing they didn't believe in panties either. He later found out his guess was correct.

As he got up to go meet the roommate, Buck asked Donna, "Don't you even want to know my name?"

Donna smiled, "Cowboy will do for now. Let's see how you do before we would want to go to any trouble."

Donna's roommate introduced herself as Rhonda. Rhonda didn't ask his name either. She was also content to call him Cowboy. When they got to the girls' apartment, Buck and Rhonda adjourned to her bedroom and shucked their clothes. Buck thought it was curious that Rhonda didn't shut her door. Most women wanted their privacy.

Rhonda shocked Buck. She reached her first pinnacle of ecstasy during foreplay. It didn't stop there. She reached another peak about every five minutes. Buck had never had a woman respond like that. When Rhonda was completely exhausted and spent, she whispered, "Cowboy, what's your name?"

Buck beamed, "The name's Buck, ma'am, and don't you forget it."

As Rhonda drifted off to sleep, she murmured, "You don't have to worry about that, Cowboy… I mean Buck. I'll remember."

Buck didn't bother to put his clothes back on. He just exited Rhonda's open door and entered Donna's open door. He climbed into bed with the naked Donna. She was feigning sleep as Buck whispered in her ear, "I'm pretty sure Rhonda is no longer sad."

Donna smiled, acknowledging she was awake. "So, I heard."

Buck climbed on top of her. "I think you need a little reward for being such a good friend."

Donna welcomed him. "I agree. I deserve it."

THE FIRST RIDE

Buck hauled Buttermilk back to his hundred-acre ranch located west of Ft. Worth. It was already a horse facility when he bought it, complete with barns, corrals, turn-out paddocks and run-in sheds. The only other horses at the ranch were four saddle horses he and his friends used for riding.

The house was not a mansion, but a comfortable, three bedroom, two story brick with 3,500 square feet of living space and an attached three-car garage. Two hundred yards from the main house was a small trailer house that could be used by the hired help. Buck sold the trailer the first week. It triggered too many bad memories.

Buck was right about Buttermilk being spirited. The problem was the colt was way over the line. He was rambunctious and borderline downright mean. Even though he was just a colt, it took the help of four other men at the sale to get Buttermilk loaded into the trailer for the trip home.

After giving him a couple of days to settle in, Buck began Buttermilk's training. Buttermilk fought him at every turn. If Buck wanted him to go right, he went left. If Buck wanted him to speed up, he slowed down. When Buck was at his wit's end, he called some of his trainer friends. Everyone gave the same advice: "Even if he makes a great race horse, he's not gonna be worth much in the breeding shed. He's just not bred well enough. Your best shot of making something out of him is to geld him."

Buck made up his mind and called the vet to come out and geld Buttermilk. After Buttermilk healed from the gelding, Buck started back with his training. Buttermilk was still headstrong, but at least he was now manageable.

Buck waited until Buttermilk was two years of age before starting him under saddle to ride. Buck knew a lot of trainers started riding their young horses as yearlings, but he didn't want to run the risk of injury to Buttermilk. Besides, Buck was doing well financially with his poker winnings and was not under any pressure to earn money from his one-horse stable.

Buck hired Ramon Rodriguez as his exercise rider. Ramon worked at a local training track where Buck was now stabling Buttermilk. The first time Ramon rode Buttermilk out to the track to work him, the colt stopped dead still at the entrance and watched the other horses gallop around the oval.

Ramon encouraged Buttermilk to move ahead, finally resorting to a mild tap on his hindquarters with a short whip and gently tickling his ribs with a spur. Buttermilk paid no attention to Ramon. Ramon said to Buck, who was standing by the rail watching, "Mr. Buck, he won't move. The horse has balked! What do you want me to do?"

Buck knew that Ramon was really asking if he should use the whip and spurs more vigorously. Buck was no Pollyanna. While he didn't believe in abusing animals, Buck also knew that a disobedient horse was a dangerous animal. Buck replied, "Let's just hold up for a minute. It's his first time on the track. Give him a little more time."

Eventually, Buttermilk joined the other horses and began circling the track. Buck figured that with more experience, Buttermilk would stop balking whenever he stepped on the track. Buck was wrong. Every time for the rest of his life, Buttermilk balked when he first entered the track. Ultimately, Buck came to the conclusion that the race track was Buttermilk's kingdom. The horse stopped to regally survey his territory and his subjects. When Buttermilk was satisfied, he would run. Buttermilk was happiest when he was running.

Later, Buck told Ramon, "Ramon, you don't have to call me Mr. Buck. You can just call me Buck."

Ramon shook his head, "No, Mr. Buck, I cannot do that. My father always taught to call any man who deserves respect 'mister.' My father would not be happy with me if I called you Buck."

LITTLE TIMMY

When Buck was preparing Buttermilk for his first race, two men paid him a visit while he was brushing the colt. The men seemed friendly and one extended his hand. "How you doing, Mr. Morgan? I'm Claude Barker and this is my brother, Babe. We got a little business proposition for you."

After shaking their hands, a puzzled Buck asked, "How can I help you?"

Claude grinned. "We know you got your horse entered in the race on Saturday. We want you to tell your jockey to hold him back, gives our horse a better chance to win. We'll make it worth your while."

Buck was astonished. "Are you telling me that you want me to throw the race?"

Claude nodded, "That's exactly what we're telling you!"

The Barker brothers were blights on humanity. Claude was thin with a dark olive complexion. His thick eyebrows, narrow mouth and squeaky voice reminded most of a rat. Only one person had ever pointed out to Claude that he favored a rat. That person mysteriously disappeared and was never heard from again. Claude became known as Chopper for his talent with a hand axe.

Herman appeared to be obese, but was thickly muscled under a layer of fat. He had fair features with sandy brown hair and a pleasant face. Herman was called Babe because his weapon of choice was a Louisville Slugger. The brothers routinely chopped and bludgeoned anyone who gave them even the slightest provocation.

Both men were renowned womanizers with a sadistic twist. Each was free to pork any female he fancied, but the woman was not allowed to associate with another man. Most of their harem were known as low-rent bitches hanging out in seedy bars and nightclubs. Instead of being repelled, the violent reputations of Chopper and Babe acted as an attractant to some women. The women's low self-esteem was fed by being seen in the company of the notorious men, no matter how briefly.

Babe happened to witness Timmy, a boy just barely out of high school, leaving the apartment of one of his girls. Of course the fact that Babe was exiting the apartment of a one-night stand of his own had no bearing on his rage. Babe burst in the door, screaming, "Rosie, you dirty, slutty whore! Who was that boy who just left here?"

Rosie stammered, "N..N..Now Babe, just calm down. He weren't nothing. He's a good boy. I used to know his momma. She wanted him to come by and see how I was doin'."

Rosie was a skinny, strawberry blonde. On some women freckles are attractive. On Rosie they added to an already unappealing appearance. Because she had always felt she had been shorted in the looks department, Rosie compensated by being promiscuous. She had her first sexual encounter at twelve years of age with her Uncle Frank, who was always teasing her about being ugly. At fourteen she contracted her first case of the clap. When Uncle Frank began having a painful time urinating, his doctor diagnosed the sexual disease. After a jumbo shot of penicillin, he returned to the trailer house he shared with his junkie sister, Anita who was Rosie's mother, and Rosie.

Frank grabbed Rosie by the throat and shook the slight girl like a terrier shaking a mouse. "You little bitch, I'll teach you to be screwing around on me!" Frank then beat Rosie unconscious. Before she passed out, Rosie looked with pleading eyes at her mother to help her. Her mother shrugged in a drugged stupor, "Girl, you need to listen to your uncle. He's just trying to help you out."

Babe slapped Rosie so hard, she still had a bruise two weeks later. "You lying whore! I want to know who he is or I will bash your skull in right here!" The truth was Rosie had enticed young Timmy to leave the Longhorn bar and come home with her the previous night. She spent most of the night teaching him everything he needed to know about pleasing a woman in bed.

Rosie took one look at Babe's ball bat as he gently swung it back and forth before she blurted out, "I didn't wanna do nothing! That kid might not look like much, but he's plenty strong! He made me, Babe! The little sonovabitch raped me!"

Just before he slapped her again, Babe asked, "What's the bastard's name and where can I find him?"

Rosie whimpered, "His name is Timmy Duncan. I ain't got no idea where he lives. Make him pay, Babe, for what he done to me."

Babe didn't believe for a minute that the boy raped Rosie. What pissed off Babe was the boy should have known that Rosie was his property. As Babe stomped out to get in his Cadillac, he muttered to himself, "That's what's wrong with this damn country. The damn kids don't respect nothing."

The next night Timmy was back at the Longhorn, hoping to get with Rosie again. When Rosie didn't show, Timmy left the bar to go home. As he walked across the parking lot he heard, "Hey punk!" When Timmy turned around, he saw the enraged face of Babe Barker. Babe swung his bat from his heels, striking Timmy's ribcage, bones crunching loudly. Babe beat Timmy to a bloody pulp in full view of a dozen witnesses going into or leaving the Longhorn. When the police questioned everyone later, no one saw anything or knew of anyone who did.

The doctor at the ER told Timmy's parents when they arrived that their son only had a fifty-fifty chance of survival. Timmy pulled through, but only after spending over a month in the hospital with another six months of physical therapy. Timmy was never the same physically after the beating. Worse, his spirit was broken. He lived with the memory of the merciless whipping every day for the rest of his life.

Babe then disciplined Rosie by inviting a dozen of his cronies to her apartment. The gang of men entered her apartment with Babe ordering, "Rosie, strip off all your damn clothes and get on the bed!" While Babe stood watch with his bat on his shoulder as casually as a baseball player standing in the on-deck circle, each of the men used her body in any and every way imaginable. When everyone had their fill, Babe made the woman show her appreciation to the men for her "good time" by kissing the back of their hand and telling each of them, "Thank you!" Incredibly, this episode didn't trigger Rosie's intense hatred of Babe. In a twisted way, it actually enhanced her affection for him.

GIVING THE FINGER

Chopper's favorite pastime was lopping off fingers from those who had earned his displeasure. Anyone who wanted to work for him had to show their loyalty by agreeing to have one finger, up to the first knuckle, hacked off by Chopper. If any of his gang did not perform up to Chopper's expectations, they lost another joint from a finger.

After serving two stretches in the federal penitentiary in Huntsville and scuffling to just to make a living, Slick Johnson thought the financial rewards of being in the Barker gang was worth a finger or two. After he lost all the joints in two fingers to errors of judgment—according to Chopper—Slick didn't want any more of the cheese. He just wanted out of the trap.

Slick cautiously approached Chopper about resigning. "Boss, I've had a few things come up with my family I need to tend to. As much as I hate it, I'm going to need to step away from the gang for a little while, if that's all right with you. I'll be back before you know it."

Chopper studied Slick's face for a moment, finally recognizing he was looking at a man who had lost his nerve. Chopper knew he could no longer rely on Slick to do what needed to be done, so he squeaked, "Hey, my friend, I completely understand. Man's got to look out for his family. The only thing is you got to buy your way out. If I let just anybody walk away from the gang, pretty soon I wouldn't have no soldiers. A general can't operate with no soldiers."

Slick nervously replied, "Well, boss, I'll try to pay what you want. How much is it?"

Chopper chuckled. "Now Slick, I think you know what the price is."

Slick stuttered, "A… a… fin… finger?"

Chopper answered as he motioned towards a small table in the room, "Yep! Now put out the finger you want to pay with on that table. We'll get this over with and you'll be as free as a bird!"

Slick edged over to the table and reluctantly laid one finger on the table. He knew he was past the point of no return. If he tried to back out now, he knew Chopper would just as soon kill him as look at him. Slick closed his eyes as Chopper raised his axe over his head and started the downward motion. Slick screamed in shock and terror as he saw that it wasn't just his finger but his whole hand flopping around on the table. Chopper had cut his hand off at the wrist. Slick's stump was spurting blood six feet across the room.

Chopper had been sprayed with Slick's blood when he exclaimed, "Well, I'll be damned! I can't believe I missed your finger that much! That's just not right! Right now, you're a little lop-sided, Slick. I need to fix that!" Chopper nodded at a couple of his men. They held Slick's other arm on the table. Chopper severed his other hand, "Now see there! I done fixed it! You ain't lop-sided no more!"

Chopper told the other two gang members, "Take this piece of shit somewhere and finish the job. Get him out of my sight!"

The local police gave up on reining in the two gangsters, as none of the charges filed ever stuck. Either the victim disappeared or recanted his story. The local police chief asked his team of detectives, "Do you mean to tell me that we can't gather any evidence from all the crimes that the Barker gang commits?"

The head of detectives shook his head. "We can come up with evidence. The problem is it is all circumstantial, nothing that would hold up in court. We need witnesses. The Barkers don't leave witnesses. They either kill them or cause them to fear for their lives."

THE FIRST RACE

B uck responded indignantly to Claude, "You boys are barking up the wrong tree! I'm not throwing the race!"

Claude blustered, "Just do what you're told! If you screw us on this deal, you won't like what happens next!" As he stomped off, Claude turned and threatened, "Remember what I said, Morgan!"

That night Buck called Ace and related the whole story. Ace said, "Hang tight. Let me see what I can do."

The next morning, Ace called Buck back. "I called in a couple of favors from some connected wise guys. They said they'll make sure that the Barkers are told to stand down this time, but that those boys are loose cannons. My guys say they're not sure if they can control them in the future."

The race that Saturday was at Lone Star Park in Grand Prairie. After looking through the list of available jockeys, Buck decided to let Ramon ride Buttermilk in the race because Ramon seemed to get along with the horse, even though he couldn't make Buttermilk do anything that Buttermilk didn't want to do.

Buck had begun affectionately calling the stubborn Buttermilk, Butthead. As they were tacking Buttermilk in the saddling paddock, Buck stroked the horse's neck, whispering, "You gonna run today, Butthead? I hope you're not planning to embarrass us."

The sky was foreboding with dark clouds threatening rain, but so far the race track was dry. Buck hoped the rain held off long enough to get in Buttermilk's race.

Before boosting Ramon into the saddle, Buck gave him a series of instructions on how to run the race. Ramon's face said, *really?* Buck realized his directions were a waste of time when it came to managing Buttermilk. Finally he said, "Oh hell—just try to stay on top of him."

Carol had flown up from Houston for the race. Buck had asked her, "Would you wear that yellow sundress for the race?"

Carol replied, "Okay, but why that particular dress?"

Buck mischievously grinned. "Because I got lucky once when you were wearing that dress. I want to see if it works for a second time."

Carol squealed as she slapped him on the shoulder. "Buck!"

Buck joined Carol on the rail at the finish line. Carol had never seen Buck be anything but calm, cool and collected. She was slightly shocked and a little amused to see that he was very nervous. Carol slipped her hand in his and gave Buck a reassuring squeeze.

The race was a maiden race for two-year-old horses that had not won at the track. It had a large field of ten entries. It took more time than normal to get all the young horses loaded for the three-quarter-mile race. Once all the horses were in the starting gates, the bell rang and the gates simultaneously jerked open.

Buck had been pleased that Buttermilk had drawn the four hole. He thought that was a good place to start. Buck definitely didn't want on the extreme inside or outside. Buck had his binoculars trained on the starting gate. When the gates opened and all the horses boiled out, Buck was dismayed that Buttermilk just stood in the gate while the other horses were putting plenty of real estate between themselves and Buttermilk.

Buck screamed at the top of his lungs, "Damn you, Butthead! Run, you son-of-a-bitch, run!" Buttermilk casually loped out as Ramon was also screaming and spanking him on the hip. The announcer intoned in an amused voice, "It looks like Bold Buttermilk has decided to join us."

Buttermilk went from a slow lope into an all-out sprint. He was an exceptionally gifted racehorse. Some horses hit the ground in bone jarring fashion when they run. Buttermilk almost floated over the earth, even at full stride.

As he picked up speed, Carol was jumping up and down, shouting, "Run, Buttermilk! Run!"

Buck had quit yelling and had accepted the inevitability of the outcome. He muttered, "Yeah, he's finally running, but he's too far back. That damn Butthead is still gonna finish in last place."

The announcer gave the status of each horse starting with the one in the lead and finishing with Buttermilk, "Bold Buttermilk has made up considerable ground, but still trails the field by ten lengths." The Barker brothers' horse, Flying Pegasus, had a comfortable two-length lead over the second-place horse.

As they made the turn for the stretch run to the finish line, the loudspeaker blared, "And it's still Flying Pegasus out in front by two lengths. Wait a minute! Bold Buttermilk has caught the pack and is making a move!"

Buttermilk went around the outside, which was the longest route, but avoided the other horses. His stride was a thing of beauty. Buck and Ramon knew how talented Buttermilk was, but had no idea if they could harness his athletic ability.

The announcer was caught up in the drama on the track. "Flying Pegasus is still out front, but Bold Buttermilk has moved up to a length and a half behind him and is closing fast! With half a furlong to go, they are neck and neck! It's Flying Pegasus! It's Bold Buttermilk! It's Flying Pegasus! It's Bold Buttermilk! It's a photo finish, folks! It's too close to call!"

During the stretch run, Buck and Carol had abandoned any shred of decorum and were screeching, urging Buttermilk on. They now waited tensely for the stewards to review the picture and declare the winner. Their decision was known when Buttermilk's number was put up as the winner. Buttermilk had won by half a nostril.

A jubilant Buck and Carol were hugging and laughing as they hurried to the winner's circle for the official picture. Buttermilk and a broadly smiling Ramon were already there. Buck asked Ramon, "What happened out there?"

Ramon smiled even wider. "I did what you told me, Mr. Buck. I stayed on top of him." Ramon leaned over and patted Buttermilk, "He is a *mucho* race horse."

Buck was rubbing Buttermilk's muzzle while Carol was fawning over him, cooing and making baby talk. Buck was still stroking Buttermilk's nose as he spoke to the horse, "All right, you got away with that crazy shit today, but you were lucky. You gotta start listening to what we tell you. You might just make a great racehorse, but you won't if you don't listen to us."

Buck didn't believe that horses could express human emotions, but the look in Buttermilk's eye had to be a smirk.

Ramon dismounted and Buck snapped a lead on Buttermilk's bridle. He said to Carol, "We're going to take care of Buttermilk, but I have a table reserved in the clubhouse. Just ask the staff to seat you there. Ace should be there too. I'll be there shortly."

On the trip back to the barn, Chopper and Babe Barker were waiting on them. Buck returned their menacing glare, but continued on to Buttermilk's stall without acknowledging them. Buck had a bad feeling in the pit of his stomach about the Barker brothers. He knew that one day he was going to have to deal with them once and for all.

After getting Buttermilk cooled off, rubbed down, fed and watered, Buck asked Ramon, "Would you spend the night in Buttermilk's stall for an extra $500? Before you answer, you need to know that I want you armed."

Ramon nodded his head, "*Si*, Mr. Buck. I have a *pistola* hidden in the tack room. Is it because of those two men?"

Buck looked down the barn aisle. The Barkers were gone. "Yes, Ramon. Those are the Barker brothers. They are some bad dudes. I am going to have dinner with Carol and Ace. I will be back afterwards and stay the night with you."

Ramon reassured, "Don't you worry, Mr. Buck. I will take good care of Buttermilk."

Buck didn't mention the Barker brothers at dinner in front of Carol. There wasn't anything she could do about them so there was no reason to worry her. When they were finished with dinner, he lied to her. "Baby, I didn't like the way Buttermilk looked when I left. I think I'm gonna stay at the barn tonight just to be on the safe side. I have us a room at the Hilton. Can you catch a cab there? I will try to join you later, but I can't promise anything."

Carol sighed, "Yes, I can do that. I wanted to be with you, but I understand. You need to be sure Buttermilk is okay." Buck kissed

Carol good night and couldn't help noticing her ass as she walked off. He briefly considered going back to the hotel with her first and then going to the barn. Buck reluctantly rejected that idea because it wouldn't be fair to Ramon.

Ace said, "I'll go with you to the barn. I won big on Buttermilk today. I need to check on my golden goose. I damn sure don't want him to stop shittin' out those golden eggs."

As they walked to the barn, Ace wasn't fooled by Buck's lie. "It those damn Barkers, isn't it?"

Buck replied, "They were waiting on us at the barn after the race. They didn't say or do anything, but I know they're going to do something. Tomorrow, I'm going to hire 24-hour security for Buttermilk. Ramon is standing guard and he has a gun. I also have my .38. I kind of wish they would just show up so I could shoot the shit out of them and get all this over with."

That night was quiet. Quiet days stretched into quiet weeks, quiet weeks into quiet months. There was no sign or any further threats from the Barkers. Still, Buck maintained the 24-hour security protection on Buttermilk.

THE MASTERSON GAME

A month after the race, Cheryl surprised Buck when he was visiting Carol. Cheryl unwrapped a painting of the picture from the winner's circle when Buttermilk won his first race. Carol exclaimed, "Oh Cheryl! That is beautiful!"

Buck marveled at the realism of the beaming Carol, Buck and Ramon captured in oil. She had even managed to replicate Buttermilk's look of disdain at being kept from his oats by this trivial crap. Buck hugged Cheryl and kissed her cheek. "Thanks, Cheryl. That may be the best present I've ever gotten." Then Buck held Cheryl out at arm's length as he referenced the kiss on the cheek. "Now, Cheryl, you don't consider that kiss as us having sex, do you?" Cheryl gave him several half-hearted slaps on the chest as Carol giggled.

Buck called Ace on the phone, "Hey Ace, I got a message inviting me to a poker game at the Dallas Petroleum Club. From what I understand, it's a weekly, cash, high-stakes game. What do you think?"

Ace grunted, "I don't know about that, boy. Chris Masterson runs that game. I think you're in over your head with him. It's not going to be an honest game."

Buck snorted, "C'mon Ace, I didn't just ride into town last night on a load of turnips. If they're stacking or dealing seconds, I'll know it. Hell, you taught me how to spot that kind of shit."

Ace grumbled, "Boy, I'm telling you those guys will deal you second best hands and you'll never see it, even with what I've taught you."

Buck protested, "Bullshit! I'm just as good as they are!"

Ace replied, "Boy, I wouldn't trade you for nobody when it comes to playing your cards, but this is different. Let me tell you what's gonna happen. You're going to win a few hands and start to get comfortable. One of them boys is going to want to bet with you that he can make the jack of diamonds jump out of the deck and spit cider in your ear. As soon as you make your bet, damn well be sure you're gonna end up with an ear full of cider."

Buck laughed, "Ace, you're getting scared in your old age. I hear that there is a lot of money at play in that game. I'm going to bring some of it home. Don't worry, I got this."

Chris Masterson had made a small fortune fleecing gamblers at his rigged card games. Masterson's games always provided the finest liquor, food, girls and drugs. All of his victims were impressed by the first-class treatment they got. Most of them never made the connection that the cost of all the comforts was actually coming out of their own pockets.

Masterson had once run a small casino on the Vegas strip. He calculated that he could own his own small operation and make ten times the money, even after paying off the local police and politicians.

When Buck checked in at the front desk of the Petroleum Club, he was escorted to a private room where the card game was already in process. The room had the finest of furnishings, a marble floor, leather couches and chairs, and two crystal chandeliers. It also came complete with a bar, bartender and waitress.

A steely-eyed man strode over with a big smile as he extended his hand. "Howdy, Buck! I'm Chris Masterson. I've heard a lot about you. I'm glad to finally meet you!"

Buck shook his hand. "Well, Mr. Masterson, I appreciate you inviting me."

Masterson looked over his shoulder, then turned back to Buck. "Hell, I just had to check to see if my daddy had come in. He's the only Mr. Masterson I know!" Masterson laughed before continuing, "Just call me plain ol' Chris."

Buck grinned. "Chris it is."

When Buck took his chair at the poker table, he started pulling banded bundles of hundred dollar bills from the bank bag he was carrying. Masterson put up a hand to stop him. "Not necessary, my friend. Your credit's good here. We'll settle up at the end of the game."

Buck was a little concerned when he realized that each player could name his game of choice when it came his turn in the rotation. Most of the players chose Hold 'Em, but a few liked to play Low Ball. Low Ball is a seven card stud poker game with two cards down and five up, just like Hold 'Em. The difference is the Low Ball winner is the one with the lowest cards. The best hand in Low Ball is a wheel, ace through five. Buck sloughed it off, as he figured he was an expert at Low Ball too.

Buck won several hands of Hold 'Em and a couple of Low Ball. The player that Buck beat in Low Ball was Larry Mancil. Mancil was a professional gambler specializing in poker and horse racing, although he was also a degenerate who would bet on anything. He had won and lost millions of dollars over the years.

After each hand that Mancil lost to Buck, he would say, "Nice hand, Buck. Well played." There was just something about Mancil that seemed a little off-kilter to Buck's sixth sense. In the next hand of Low Ball, Buck caught 6-4-3-2-ace in the first five cards. It was a powerful hand second only to a wheel.

Buck bet moderately until he felt he had the best hand. He then checked and gave Mancil the lead in betting, hoping to trap him. Mancil bet on the sixth card with Buck just smooth-calling him. On the last card, Buck checked, then raised Mancil's bet $10,000.00. Mancil called and Buck flipped over his cards, showing the 6-4.

Mancil gave a low whistle. "Man, that's just outhouse luck. Sorry, man." Mancil revealed his wheel and raked in the pot. It was Buck's turn to say, "Good hand."

There was one thing that didn't make any sense at all to Buck. Mancil had the nuts on the hand. Why didn't he re-raise Buck? Buck recalled Ace telling him that a good hustler never broke his pigeon. He would bleed them a little at a time.

The next time around the table, Mancil selected Low Ball as the game. It was no surprise since that had been his choice every time it was his turn. This time it took Buck six cards before he had another 6-4. He checked each time, but called each of Mancil's bets. When Mancil checked to him after the last card, Buck didn't fall for the trap and just turned over his hole cards, displaying his

6-4. Just as he suspected, Mancil turned over another wheel and dragged the pot.

Mancil faked a show of concern. "Don't worry, buddy. You just had a little run of bad luck." Buck smiled at him as he studied Mancil's face. Buck thought, *For having the reputation for being so smart, these are some dumb sons of bitches for dealing me two second best hands in a row.*

Buck abruptly pushed up from his chair. "Well, boys, I've got to be shoving off. I've got to get up early in the morning. Deal me out."

Masterson bounded to his feet from the wingback leather chair where he had been observing the game. "Hey Buck, don't run off. The night's still young. What can I get you? A drink? A little dope? We got the best there is. How about a girl? We got the best there too."

Buck laughed. "No thanks, Mr. Masterson. I'm good. Thanks for inviting me. I'll just settle up and be on my way."

Masterson responded, "Hey, it's Chris, remember. You don't have to pay me tonight. I'll carry you till next week's game."

Buck replied, "I appreciate it, but I'm a cash-and-carry guy. I will pay now." Buck had no intention of ever coming back.

After the game had ended for the night, Masterson called Mancil and the dealer into his office. Masterson was in a rage when he spoke to the dealer, "What the hell am I paying you big money for? That's the stupidest shit I've ever seen, to deal the man two big second hands in a row! Your ass is fired! And, you're damn lucky I don't put a bullet through that thick skull of yours."

On the drive back to the ranch, Buck speed dialed Ace on his cell. Ace answered, "How'd it go, Hot Shit?"

Buck ruefully replied, "My damn ear is full of cider."

Ace chuckled, "I'm willing to bet that it was pretty damn expensive cider too."

A subdued Buck grumbled, "Expensive enough."

Ace pointed out, "I reckon the next time, you'll listen to what ol' Ace has to say!"

Buck muttered, "Shut up."

TWINS

Buck now saw Carol every weekend. Sometimes she flew to DFW where Buck would pick her up and drive her to the ranch. Sometimes Buck flew to Houston where Carol would pick him up and take him back to her and Cheryl's apartment.

Normally, most couple's love affairs begin to cool off after a time. Buck and Carol were not on any downward slide in the love department. In fact, it was growing hotter every time they were together. Their firecracker made a louder boom every time it was lit. Once Cheryl hollered from the next room, "Do you guys ever give it a rest? Keep it up and you're both are going to have to go into Pep Boys and get your genitals relined!"

Carol giggled, "Sorry, Cheryl, we'll try to keep it down!"

Buck whispered to Carol, "And what exactly are you going to keep down? If it's what I think you're talking about, you're never going to keep it down for long."

Carol softly chortled as she put her hand over Buck's mouth, "Hush." Carol slipped her hand away from Buck's lips and kissed him. The kiss deepened. They couldn't stop themselves from starting a new session of lovemaking.

When Buck was in Houston, he and the twins were usually a threesome when they went to eat, to the movies or any type of event. Sometimes Cheryl brought a date, but most of the time she went single. Buck would tease Cheryl, "No date again? If you quit being so scary, more guys would go out with you!"

Cheryl retorted, "Shut your ass, Buck Morgan! You don't know what you're talking about! I can't help it if I'm picky!"

Buck replied, "See, that's exactly what I'm talking about!"

In spite of them good-naturedly ragging on each other, they developed a strong brother-sister bond between the two of them. Carol usually ended up laughing the hardest at their point-counterpoint exchanges.

When Carol was at the ranch, Buck said, "You know it would be all right when you come here to invite Cheryl along."

Carol flashed her megawatt smile. "You love Cheryl, don't you?"

Buck paused before answering reluctantly, "Well… I guess I do, but Dear God in Heaven, don't tell her I said that! I would never hear the end of it!"

THE RECORD RUN

After Buttermilk broke his maiden at Lone Star, Buck laid him off for a month. Because he was a young horse, Buck decided to play it totally safe with Buttermilk's health. Buttermilk was healthy and sound. Buck wanted to keep him that way. His only exercise was being led around the exercise track by Ramon riding another horse. Buttermilk did not like it. He would kick and buck, wanting to run. The big, muscular Appaloosa was especially chosen for his size and calm nature to be a "pony" horse. Ramon and the App ponied Buttermilk every day. The App would just quietly muscle the rambunctious Buttermilk around the track. Finally, even Buttermilk submitted to being ponied.

Buck targeted an allowance race at Remington Park in Oklahoma City for Buttermilk's return to the track. The date of the race would fit perfectly in Buttermilk's training schedule to get him ready to run. In an allowance race, the track adds money to the purse.

Three days before the race, Buck and Ramon trailered Buttermilk to Remington Park and stabled him in the stall that had been reserved for him when Buck entered him in the race. This would give Buck a couple of days to get Buttermilk comfortable with his new surroundings.

The week before, when they were still at the ranch, Buck was checking the entries to see if any additional horses had been entered. A rock formed in the pit of his stomach when he read the newest entry: Flying Pegasus, Barker Brothers Stable.

Buck told Ramon the news. Ramon responded, "Mr. Buck, maybe we should scratch Buttermilk from that race and run him somewhere else."

Buck clenched his teeth. "The hell I will! I'm not running from those two sons of bitches! They can kiss my ass!"

Ramon hedged, "Mr. Buck, those are *hombres muy malo*! Please think about it."

Buck was determined. "Nope, we're going!"

The day before the race, the Barkers strode down the aisle of the barn where Buttermilk was stalled. Chopper had a sick grin on his face when he saw Buck. "Morgan, I'm gonna get right to the point. We let you skate on that other race because a man who we do a lot of business with asked us real nicely to give you a pass. That's not gonna happen this time! You don't hold that damn horse of yours tomorrow, you're gonna pay the price!"

Buck was fighting mad. "My answer is still the same, jackass! You boys get away from me and my horse or I will stick your skinny ass up your brother's fat ass!"

Chopper and Babe were bristling, wanting to kill Buck then and there, but they realized there were too many witnesses. As they stomped off, Babe yelled, "You've been warned!"

Race day was a typical fall day in Oklahoma, bright with sunshine, but crisp with a slight chill requiring a light jacket. Buck momentarily forgot about the Barkers. The day made him glad to be alive.

Buck and Carol were on the rail at the finish line right before the race started. Buck nervously whispered to Carol, "I hope Butthead doesn't wait again until everybody's out of sight before he decides to leave the gate this time."

Carol hugged him. "Don't worry, honey. Buttermilk's going to do great! You got to have a little faith in him."

Buck replied, "I do have faith in him. I have faith that the hardhead will figure out a way to screw this up."

The bell to start the race suddenly rang and the horses broke from the gates. Buck slapped his binoculars to his eyes, dreading the sight of Buttermilk still lounging in the gate. Buck was shocked at what he saw! Buttermilk was first out of the gate and was sprinting away from the other horses.

After first, he was ecstatic about the start, then Buck became horrified and began yelling, "No! No! That's too fast! Ramon, pull him up! He can't last at that speed! Pull him up!" Every spectator at Remington Park could see Ramon standing in his stirrups and desperately sawing on the reins, trying to get the runaway under control. It was no use. Buttermilk had the bit in his teeth and his neck rigid.

The announcer chuckled sarcastically, "Folks, it looks like Bold Buttermilk wants to set a new track record." Every person watching the race knew that the crazy horse was going out way too fast and would have to shut down from exhaustion with most of the race still left to be run. No way could he maintain that speed for the three-quarter mile.

Buck handed the binoculars to Carol and buried his face in his hands, using his index fingers to massage his temples. The announcer continued to call the race, expecting at any minute for Buttermilk to slow down and probably have to walk to the finish line.

The loudspeakers boomed, "And Bold Buttermilk has opened up a 20-length lead on the field. Flying Pegasus is trying desperately to close the gap!" The announcer went through the status of the rest of the pack.

The announcer continued, "And down the stretch they go! Folks, we may be witnessing history today!" Buck lifted his head to watch the stretch run. He couldn't believe it. Buttermilk had settled into a ground-eating stride that was still fast, but not as fast as the first part of the race. It was fast enough that none of the other horses could cut down the gap Buttermilk had created.

"It's Bold Buttermilk by 20 lengths! Bold Buttermilk by 20 lengths! It's Bold Buttermilk at the finish! If the race stands, it's a new track record!" The announcer gave the finish for the rest of the field, but no one could hear it. All the spectators were standing and screaming! After a preliminary check by the stewards, Buttermilk's number was put up as the winner. The announcer blared, "It's official, folks! Bold Buttermilk has set a new record time for three-quarter mile at Remington Park!"

Buck and Carol barely made it to the winner's circle as Buck had to push their way through a cheering crowd. People were wanting to shake their hands and pat them on the back. Buck and Carol were now local celebrities.

When they got to the winner's circle, Ramon grinned at Buck. "I stayed on top of him again!"

Buck laughed heartily, "Yes, you did! Yes, you did, my friend!" As Buck looked over the sea of adoring faces, one scowling face stood out. Buck locked eyes with Chopper Barker. Chopper used his finger to make a slitting motion across his throat.

Carol saw the look of concern cross Buck's face. "What is it, honey? Is there something wrong?"

Buck forced a smile. "It's nothing, baby. How could anything be wrong on a day like today?" Buck whirled her around and gave Carol a long kiss. The crowd yelled even louder.

Buttermilk's race was immediately picked up by the national media. The race was the lead story for ESPN that night. Everyone was singing the praises of Buttermilk, who was being referred to as Superhorse. Everyone also wanted to know how in the hell did Buttermilk get his name?

At a back table in a local bar, Chopper seethed, "If that sonovabitch thinks he can screw us over, he's gotta another think coming!"

Babe chimed in, "Hell, the bastard's done it twice now. Brother, we gotta teach this prick a lesson he'll never forget!"

Chopper raged, "Killing him is just too easy. I want him to suffer, really suffer!"

Babe asked, "Have you got any good ideas?"

Chopper smirked, "Yeah, I got a great idea. It involves that bitch he's been banging. When we get done with her, he'll be kissing our ass or anything else we want him to kiss!" Babe raised his eyebrows and snickered.

THE TEXT MESSAGE

Two weeks later, Cheryl parked her car in the apartment's parking lot. She scarcely noticed an unfamiliar white van with darkened windows parked close to her. Cheryl was closing her car door when a man roughly grabbed her, putting his hand over her mouth while a second man shoved a bag over her head. Both men dragged the struggling girl into the back of the van.

When the van started up, the first man pulled his hand away from her mouth underneath the bag. Chopper threatened, "Keep your mouth shut, do what you're told and you won't get hurt!" Cheryl sobbed quietly.

The van slowed down and Cheryl heard what sounded like a garage door open and shut behind them as they drove through. The van stopped and Cheryl was jerked out by one arm. When they pulled off the bag on her head, she could see they were in an old, dilapidated warehouse. The boarded-up windows said the warehouse had been abandoned.

Cheryl was badly frightened. "What do you want from me?"

Chopper backhanded her, splitting her lip. "I done told you once to shut up! I ain't telling you again!"

Babe chimed in, "That damn boyfriend of yours thought he could screw us. He owes us. You get to make the first payment."

A horrified Cheryl realized the men thought she was Carol. She wanted to scream out that she wasn't Carol, that she was her sister. But Cheryl never denied that she wasn't Carol. She knew she couldn't betray her sister, no matter the consequences. The men started tearing her clothes off. Cheryl gritted her teeth and accepted her fate.

Buck and Carol were having supper at a steak house in Ft. Worth. Buck's phone buzzed with a message. When he tapped on the message, Buck saw a picture that sickened and terrified him. It was a picture that he would never be able to erase from his memory. The picture was of a naked Cheryl covered in blood from having her throat cut. The caption read, "You won't be banging this bitch no more! BB"

Buck quickly shut off his phone and stood up from the table, "Come on, Carol. We need to go, right now."

Carol was confused. "But why, Buck? What's wrong?"

Buck pulled two $100 bills from his wallet and tossed them on the table to cover their meal. Buck ordered, "Get up, Carol! Now!"

Carol could tell from the look on his face and the tone of his voice that it was something serious. As they hurried out to Buck's pickup, Carol said, "Buck, you're scaring me. Tell me what's wrong." When they were seated in the truck, Buck had a heavy sadness in his voice. "Carol, this is the hardest thing I've ever had to do. It's Cheryl… she's been killed."

Carol screamed and began to cry, "Are you sure? How do you know that? Did the message you just got say that?"

Buck leaned over and hugged her, "Baby, I wouldn't tell you something like this unless I was absolutely sure. I'm sure."

Carol demanded, "I want to see for myself! Show me the message!"

Buck shook his head. "Baby, it was a picture of Cheryl sent by the Barker brothers. It is too horrible. I will never let you see it."

Carol moaned, "I have to get to Houston. I have to see for myself."

Buck replied, "We are going to the police station to report this. They can contact the Houston police to send a squad car over to your apartment. That will be much faster than if we tried to drive down there."

Buck and Carol met with a detective with the Ft. Worth police department. After giving the detective the complete history of his problems with the Barker brothers, Buck pulled up the picture and handed his phone to the detective. The cop flinched when he saw the picture. Carol leapt from her chair and snatched the phone from his hand before he or Buck could stop her. Carol screamed, "I want to see my sister!"

When Carol's eyes focused on the picture, they rolled up in the back of her head and she fainted. Buck managed to catch her before she hit the floor. After applying cold compresses to Carol's forehead, she came to. Buck despaired at the look in her eyes. They were lifeless, zombie substitutes for the sparkling eyes that always accompanied Carol's famous smile. Buck wondered if he would ever see her smile again.

The Houston police found Cheryl's body in a dumpster behind her and Carol's apartment. The Barkers wanted to be sure that Buck got the full effect of what they thought was his girlfriend's death. An autopsy revealed that the killers had tortured Cheryl. That fact, coupled with the caption on the death picture, led to only one conclusion. Cheryl was aware that they thought she was Carol. Cheryl chose a horrible death over betraying her sister. That was almost too much for Carol to bear. "Buck they didn't know who they really had. Cheryl died for me. It should have been me! It should have been me…" Carol began to weep hysterically.

Buck was crying too as he tried to comfort Carol. "Baby, your sister is the bravest person I've ever known." Carol was inconsolable.

The police and their forensic team came up empty. No clues. The phone that was used to text the picture was a drop phone purchased at a local Walmart. A search of the surveillance cameras showed the purchaser was a homeless vagrant. While police were able to locate him, his alcoholism had rendered him barely able to identify himself, much less anybody else.

THE VEGAS REMEDY

The next few days were a blur that culminated in Buck and Carol sitting next to her grief-stricken parents at Cheryl's gravesite. A crying Irma Washington was being supported by two of the workers from New Life. Buck couldn't help but remember how Irma had charged him with taking care of the girls. When the preacher finished his benediction, Buck got Carol's arm to guide her to his pickup. Carol pulled away from his touch.

Carol surprised him. "Buck, I'm going home with my parents."

Buck responded sympathetically, "Okay, I can understand that. When do you want me to come and get you?"

Carol was more emphatic. "No, you don't understand! I don't want you to come and get me! I don't want to see you ever again!"

Buck was overwhelmed. "But... baby... why?"

Carol's eyes were narrow slits as she accused him, "You knew how dangerous those men were. You didn't even have to run Buttermilk in that race, but your pride wouldn't let you back down. If it wasn't for your stupid pride, Cheryl would be alive today. Now, stay away from me! I never want to see your face again."

Ace had come to the funeral out of respect for Carol. He overheard their conversation. Ace walked over and put his arm around the shell-shocked Buck. "Come on, boy. Give her some time. She's hurting bad. Once she thinks it over, she'll come around."

Buck disagreed. "I don't think so, Ace. She's never looked at me like that before."

Ace reassured him, "Aw, I bet she does. Come on. Let's go home."

Buck trudged to his pickup. He wanted to believe Ace was right, but in his heart, he knew Ace was wrong. Ace had flown in for the funeral. He drove the pickup for the four-hour trip back to the ranch. Buck never said a word, just stared out the window in a trance. For the next six months, Buck would not say Carol's name. It was too painful. He would refer to her as "she" or "her."

When they got to the ranch, Ace went to the barn and said privately to Ramon, "Go in the house and stay with Buck. I'm taking his truck to my townhouse. I'm gonna get some clothes and come live here for a while."

Ramon understood. "Don't worry, Mr. Ace. I'll take good care of him until you get back."

It took two days before Ace could get more than one or two words at a time from Buck. Finally Buck blurted out, "Ace, you know what the worst part of this whole deal is? Carol was exactly right! It was my fault Cheryl is dead!" Buck began to cry. "Ace, I loved Cheryl like she was my own sister, and I killed her!"

Ace objected, "Buck, you were not responsible for her death. The Barker brothers are the ones responsible, may they rot in hell! Them and only them are the guilty ones."

Buck continued to cry. Ace felt like Buck needed to get his grief out of his system so he let Buck cry until he had no more tears.

Buck tried to call Carol several times. Each time, Carol's mother asked Carol if she wanted to talk to Buck. Every time, Carol said no. The last time he tried, Mrs. Martin said, "Buck, I think it would be best for you to wait until Carol calls you."

Over the next couple of months, Buck moped around the ranch. He would go to the barn and hug Buttermilk's neck, but that was about it. Finally, Ace had enough.

Ace ordered, "Okay, this shit has gone on long enough! You had a hard knock, one of the hardest. Now, it's time to get your ass in gear and get to moving! Get some clothes packed. We're going to Vegas! You're going to play in the World Series of Poker!"

Buck listlessly replied, "Ace, I appreciate the offer, but I'm not interested in doing that."

Ace roared, "Offer? Offer? This is no damn offer! Now, shut your ass and get ready or I'll send for a couple of my boys who collect gambling debts for me and I'll have them load you up. It's your choice. Load up or I'll have you loaded up!"

Buck smiled weakly, "All right. All right. I'll pack some clothes. Damn grouchy old man."

Ace continued his tirade, "This is a down time for Buttermilk anyway. You got plenty of time to play in that tournament. I'm paying the $10,000 entry fee. We'll split any money you win, but if you lose my ten grand, I'm knocking you in the head and dumping your ass in the first bar ditch I come to. So, you better get your shit together!"

Buck grinned. Ace had been too nice to him. It was good to have the old Ace back.

Buck and Ace flew to Vegas. All the poker greats were there: Doyle "Texas Dolly" Brunson, Phil Hellmuth, Erik Seidel, Daniel Negreanu and Phil Ivey, just to name a few. When Buck greeted the poker legends, each of them called him by name. Buck was humbled and slightly amazed that they knew who he was.

Buck got the biggest kick from Doyle Brunson. The godfather of Texas Hold 'Em was revered by one and all. Whenever Brunson eliminated a player from the tournament, the player would pump Texas Dolly's hand and thank him profusely. They considered it an honor to be sent to the rail by the most famous poker player of all time. One eliminated player gushed as he left the table, "Can you believe this shit? Knocked out by Doyle Brunson! Holy crap on a cracker! I can't wait to tell the boys back home. This is a story I'm gonna be able to tell my grandkids."

Buck didn't win the World Series of Poker, but he lasted long enough to turn Ace's $10,000 into $217,000. As Buck counted out Ace's winnings, Ace grunted, "You may be worth a shit after all. What are you going to do with your hundred grand?"

Buck retorted, "Hadn't even thought about it yet. I'm just so glad I'm not being dumped in a bar ditch!"

Ace grinned, "You still need to watch your ass. We ain't home yet."

FERNANDO'S HIDEAWAY

/////////////////////

F ernando's Hideaway was a seedy bar in South Oak Cliff. The southern part of Dallas was notorious for violence and criminal activity. This bar was a cut above the others when it came to sheer evilness. It was owned by the Barker brothers. The Barkers met there every day that they were in town. They ruled their evil empire from the bar.

A wiretap in the place would have solved half the crimes in Dallas. The wiretap never happened and never would as the Barkers had two federal judges in their pocket.

One day Buck told Ace, "I'm going out on the town tonight."

Ace responded, "That's good. You need to kick up your heels a little. Where're you going?"

Buck casually replied. "Fernando's Hideaway."

Ace exploded, "Boy, have you lost what little sense you got? You know that's the Barkers main hangout! They'll kill and cut you up into little pieces. And, they'll probably cut you into little pieces before they kill you!"

Buck's face was dark and grim. "Ace, I can't live with myself any longer without doing something about the Barkers. They killed my sister, and the only woman I'll probably ever love hates me because of them. The law can't do anything about them 'cause everyone is scared shitless of them. I'm not scared of them. I'm taking my .38. I'm going to kill them or they're going to kill me. Either way, I'm going to get it settled."

Ace protested, "Son, that's not the way to handle it. It's almost a sure suicide! I got connections. Let's hire some professionals to take 'em out."

Buck gave a small smile. "Ace, I appreciate it, but I'm not hiring somebody else to do my dirty work."

Ace answered, "But, kid, that's just gonna get you killed!"

Buck nodded his head. "Maybe… I don't know if that would be all that bad a thing."

Buck leaned back in the booth at Fernando's Hideaway, slowly sipping on a cold longneck. He closed his eyes, savoring the taste of the beer. Buck snapped to attention when he heard the squeaky voice of Chopper Barker. "Well, well, well, what do we have here?"

The gravelly sound of Chopper's brother Babe declared, "Why, dear brother, I believe it's the famous Buck Morgan. Hey Buck, how's it hanging?"

Chopper commanded the patrons, the waitresses and the bartenders, "Everybody out! Everybody except our guest of honor, the great Buck Morgan." Every inhabitant of the bar scurried out without so much as a backward glance. It was common knowledge that when the Barker brothers were on the prod, the farther one could be away from them, the better.

Chopper grinned maliciously. "Your luck has finally run out, Morgan. You're about to find out what happens to them that crosses the Barker brothers."

Chopper confidently fingered his hand axe as Babe tapped the big end of his baseball bat on the palm of one hand. Buck slid out of the booth as he reached around to the small of his back and smoothly pulled his Smith & Wesson .38 Special from its holster.

Buck smirked at the gangsters as he cocked the pistol, "It's just like you two dickheads to bring an axe and a bat to a gun fight."

Babe snickered as he called back over his shoulder, "Boys!" Four more hoodlums quickly entered and spread out, each armed with a pistol or a rifle.

There was no fear in Buck's eyes, even though he was outgunned four to one and outmanned six to one. Buck said, "Well boys, it appears we have us a Mexican standoff."

Chopper sneered, "We ain't got no Messican standoff! If you ain't noticed, I'm no pepper belly! If you hadn't pulled that damn gun, we was gonna cut and whomp you to death. Now, we're just gonna shoot the shit out of ya!" Chopper paused to give Buck a chance to let it sink in what was about to happen.

When Chopper felt the time was right, he shrilly ordered his men, "Kill him!" The guns all banged at once and gun smoke clouded the air. The bullets zinged towards Buck like a swarm of deadly hornets.

As soon as Chopper said, "Kill him!" Buck dove on the floor, firing at the Barkers on his way down. His eyes went wide in astonishment when all four of the gang henchmen were blasted from behind. Buck had gotten a slug into Chopper's left shoulder and Babe's right thigh.

As the gun smoke began to clear, Buck grinned as he saw Ace and three of Ace's boys with smoke curling from the ends of their gun barrels. Ace and his men had slipped in undetected as the Barker gang was focused on killing Buck.

Ace disarmed the wounded Barker brothers as Buck regained his feet. Buck's grin grew wider. "Well, Ace, I owe you one."

Ace retorted, "One, hell! You owe me a hundred!" Ace looked at the moaning Barkers. "What are we gonna do with these turds?"

Buck said quietly, "Y'all clear out. I've got some private business with these boys." When Ace shooed his guys out, Buck added, "You too, Ace. Make sure nobody comes in until I come out."

Ace questioned, "Are you sure, boy?"

Buck nodded. "I'm sure."

The Barkers had already sunk to the floor, trying to find a position to ease their pain. Chopper squeaked, "You need to call an ambulance. Me and Babe need to see a doctor."

Buck said, "That's really not a problem, Barker. You don't need a doctor."

Chopper's eyebrows furled into a scowl. "What the hell you talking bout Morgan? Can't you see me and Babe are bleeding like stuck pigs?"

Buck studied their faces, wanting to retain this memory in his mind. "You two pond scum are not going to be feeling any pain in just a minute, although there is going to be a lot of pain first."

A look of horror spread over both Barkers. Babe stuttered, "N…N…Now hold on, Buck. We might of got out a line a little, but we can make it right. We got money… lots of it!"

Buck seethed, "You killed my sister. MY SISTER! And you tortured her! There's no amount of money that can pay for that!" Buck seized Babe's bat and hit a glancing blow off his forehead. The thump of the bat knocked Babe on his back, legs splayed. He was in a little bit of a daze until he felt the immense pain that was produced when Buck crushed his dick and balls with a mighty swing of the bat. One wouldn't think that Babe could yell any louder until Buck hit him again in his destroyed groin. Babe yelled louder.

Buck threw the bat down and picked up Chopper's axe. All the terrified Chopper could do was cry like a baby and plead, "Please... please... please!" Buck struck Chopper in the head with the flat of the axe, stunning him. Buck pushed Chopper's legs apart and swung the axe. Chopper howled like a demon and bolted upright. Chopper was aghast to see his penis and scrotum separated from the rest of his body.

Buck then put two slugs behind each of their ears, as Babe begged and Chopper cried for his mother. Thus ended the reign of terror of the Barker brothers. They went out with a bang and a whimper.

As Buck left the bar, Ace grabbed his arm. "Are you alright, boy?" Buck didn't know how to answer, so he just shrugged his shoulders. Ace pulled him away, "Come on, boy. We need to skedaddle before the fuzz gets here."

When the police arrived at the scene of the blood bath, they performed all their obligatory duties. The truth was when they identified the bodies, the cops' main feelings were relief that they no longer had to deal with the Barkers and their gang. One detective remarked during the investigation, "We need to find the bastards who did this."

Another detective was puzzled. "And why is that?"

The first detective grinned. "Because we need to give those sons of bitches a medal!"

All the major networks broke the story of the massacre in south Dallas, noting the mob ties of the victims. The organized crime "experts" for the news programs speculated that it was possibly a battle for turf in the lucrative drug market.

Giuseppe Gambino, the mob boss for the Southwest who resided in Kansas City, was asked by one of his captains, "What should we do about this, boss?"

Gambino snorted, "Not a damn thing. I was tired of dealing with those jackoffs anyway. Hell, I was thinking about whacking them myself."

A month after the killings, Ace told Buck, "I got an old buddy high up in the Dallas police department. I called him and asked if they were making any progress in the Barker deal. He told me they were pretty sure what had happened and pretty sure about who killed them. He also said that they had very little hard evidence to tie anyone to the shooting. My buddy said, short of somebody wanting to confess, they were probably done with the case."

Buck thought about it for a minute. "Did he say anything else?"

Ace replied, "Yeah, he asked me if I had anything I wanted to clear my conscious about."

Buck asked, "What did you tell him?"

Ace muttered, "I told him to kiss my ass."

CLOSING THE MOUTH

Buck played in a weekly Saturday game at the Hyatt Regency hotel at the Dallas-Ft. Worth airport. It was a game for high rollers. It had two things going for it. One, it was at the airport so it was easy to fly in and out to attend the game. Two, it was run by Ace Wiggins, so everyone knew it was an honest game and everyone would get a fair shake. Ace's reputation was impeccable.

Poker is a game of skill, but there is still a certain amount of luck that effects the outcome. Buck, like anyone who gambles for a living, had an occasional bad session. When he did, he knew he was going to get his ass ate out by Ace for any stupid plays he had made. Overall, Buck did well. He was clearing over a million dollars a year off the game.

The game was open to anyone who could pay the $100,000 buy-in. Most of the time, it was a friendly game, played by men who could afford large losses. One exception was the Saturday that Pat "The Mouth" McEnroe showed up to play.

Part of The Mouth's game was to get under the other players' skin. The best trash-talker in the NBA couldn't hold a candle to The Mouth.

The Mouth got a banker from Kansas City to fold a set of queens when The Mouth went all-in with three diamonds showing in the common cards. The banker figured The Mouth for a flush, leaving himself on the hind teat with the three queens. When the banker tossed in his cards, The Mouth flipped over his two hole cards, a seven of spades and a deuce of clubs. The Mouth chortled, "Man, where did you come from? You've got to be the worst Hold 'Em player I've ever seen. You're a complete dumb shit!" The banker turned red and steam seemed to be coming out of his ears, but since he lost, he didn't say anything.

After The Mouth won several hands against a man who owned a string of furniture stores, The Mouth laughed in his face: "I got a fifth grade girl at home that can beat your ass. Man, you suck!"

The Mouth made fun of everyone, whether they won or lost. If The Mouth won, he ridiculed the loser. If The Mouth lost, he ranted and raved about what a stupid play the winner made for even being in the pot. The Mouth said to everybody at the table, "Dear God! I hate playing with a bunch of dumb shits who don't know how to play! A smart player like myself can't figure how to play his hand because I don't know what some squirrel across the table is going to do!"

Ace called a break at the two hour mark so the players could stretch and relieve themselves. By that time there wasn't a player at the table who wasn't pissed off at The Mouth. If Ace had allowed a public discussion on killing The Mouth, there would have been a spirited debate among hanging, shooting or knifing.

Buck went to the bar. "Ace, if you don't get this sonofabitch out of here, I will shoot him stone dead!"

Ace laughed, "What's the matter, Hot Shot? Can't you handle it?"

Buck retorted, "I have never met a more arrogant prick in my life."

Ace asked, "Do you want to know how to shut his mouth up?"

Buck responded, "Right now, I'm thinking my boot down his throat or up his ass!"

Ace snorted, "No, dumbass. The only way to shut up a jackass like him is to break him."

Buck was puzzled. "Break him?"

Ace added, "Yeah, break him. Take all the sonofabitch's money. Send him home with just lint in his pockets."

When the game started back up, Buck suggested, "Gentlemen, I have a proposal. I'm pretty sure everyone is sick of this jackass's braying." Buck stared at The Mouth. "How about a little game of heads-up, just me and you. You and I both have about 250 large apiece. We play until one of us has all the cash. Let's see if your hummingbird ass can back up your alligator mouth."

The Mouth was knocked off center. He was used to being the one who did the pushing. He wasn't used to being shoved around. "Morgan, that's big talk, but I'm sure the rest of these gents want to play and not watch."

The banker exclaimed, "Go get him, Buck!"

The furniture dealer said, "Actually, I would love to see Buck kick your ass!" The rest of the players nodded their heads in agreement.

Buck grinned at The Mouth. "Well, what about it, chickenshit? You up for it or don't you have the gonads for it?"

The Mouth quickly regained his brashness, "It's your funeral, Morgan!"

Texas Hold 'Em favors the aggressive player, even more so when it's heads-up. The Mouth couldn't have been more aggressive, going all-in on every hand. Buck folded his hand every time, content to lose his ante. The Mouth was laughing at every fold. "Morgan, you gonna play a hand, or you just gonna let me ante you to death?"

Buck knew he had to draw the line somewhere. He was catching horseshit cards, but he had to take a stand. The next hand, Buck was the first to bet. He declared, "All-in."

The Mouth yelled, "Call!" and slapped down a pair of aces, a heart and a diamond. Buck reluctantly turned over a 10 of spades and a 3 of clubs. The Mouth crowed, "Nothing! The great Buck Morgan has jack shit! All I've heard is how there's a great young poker player in Texas. Well, I'd like to know where he is? It can't be this dumb sonofabitch! Morgan, don't you know any better than to try to bluff a pro like me? Stupid move from a stupid player!"

There was no more betting because all the money was already in the pot, a half a million dollars. The three card flop turned up the ace of spades, the 7 of clubs and the jack of clubs. The Mouth did a victory dance. "A set of aces, Morgan. Read 'em and weep!"

Buck replied, "It's not over yet, jackass."

The Mouth responded, "Oh, it's over! It's definitely over!"

The dealer flipped the turn card, the 10 of clubs. The Mouth calmed down a little. The rest of the players had given up hope. Now they were all at the edge of their chairs. If the board paired on the river card or showed the ace of clubs, The Mouth would crush Buck's hand with either a full house or four aces. Buck needed another club that was not the ace. If he pulled a club on the river, his flush would beat The Mouth's three aces.

For the first time, The Mouth was silent. Buck wasn't. "What's the matter, Mouth? Is your asshole starting to pucker up?" When the dealer rivered the queen of clubs, the rest of the players jumped up, yelling and shouting, and giving each other high fives.

Buck swept the huge pile of cash to his side of the table. He gloated at The Mouth, "See ya, wouldn't want to be ya!"

The Mouth grumbled, "Drew four cards to a flush. That's a little fishy, if you ask me." Ace grabbed The Mouth by the front of his shirt collar. He shoved the barrel of a Glock 9 millimeter under his chin and warned, "You better watch yourself, boy. You're about to step off into some deep shit."

The Mouth left the room and never came back, ever. After everyone left, Buck said to Ace, "I took care of him, just like you said!"

Ace growled, "You're a lucky turd and you know it!"

THE REVIVAL

After the brutal murder of their daughter, Bob and Martha Martin wondered for a while if they were going to be able to live without the ray of light that was Cheryl. Ultimately, they were able to lean on each other. While they were a long way from normalcy, their lives began to have small pleasures again.

Immediately after Cheryl's death, they focused on Carol. As devastated as they were over losing their daughter, Carol was even more so over losing her sister. Their hearts were broken all over again when Carol sobbed uncontrollably, "Mother, Dad, she died in my place. She could have told them she wasn't me, but she didn't. I wish to God that she had! I would rather be dead than living in this hell."

Martha wept silently as she stroked her daughter's hair. Bob held Carol's hand. "Honey, please don't say that. You have to go on living. We all do."

Once Bob mentioned Buck. Carol's face turned hard as flint. "I hate him! He's the reason that Cheryl's dead."

Martha said, "Carol, honey, it wasn't his fault. You know, I think that boy really loves you."

Carol got up and went to her room. "I don't want to talk about it."

Carol was morose and listless. She hadn't been in to work for two months. Bob and Martha tried to get her to go to a doctor for depression. Carol refused. Bob was at his wits' end when he decided to call Irma Washington. When he got Irma on the phone, he begged her, "Irma, we don't know where else to turn. Please come talk to Carol. Maybe you can get through to her."

Irma assured him, "I can get there in about an hour. I'll see you then."

Irma found Carol in her bedroom. Irma was shocked at Carol's appearance. She was always thin, but not this thin. Her parents could only coax her into eating a little, not enough to be healthy. Carol's skin was dull and lackluster. Her eyes were sunken back into her head. Carol had been drop-dead gorgeous. Now she was a walking cadaver.

Irma gently took Carol in her arms. "Hi, honey. How've you been?"

Carol faintly said, "I'm fine. How are you?"

Irma sat down with Carol in her lap and started to gently rock her. "Honey, I want to talk about Cheryl."

Carol's face scrunched up and she began to cry. "Irma, it should have been me. It should have been me."

Irma continued to rock her. "I know, baby. I know." When Carol's sobs settled down to sniffles, Irma said, "Let me ask you something, Carol: what do you think Cheryl would think now? What would Cheryl want you to do?"

Carol looked up at Irma. "I don't know, Irma. I really don't know."

Irma responded, "Well, I do. I know exactly what Cheryl would want. I know exactly what Cheryl would say."

Carol thought for a few moments with her chin quivering, "What Irma? What would she say?"

Irma looked Carol squarely in the eye. "She would say, 'Carol, you've spent enough time grieving for me. I'm living with God now and it's a wonderful place. But you still have work to do on Earth. There are people who need your help. I'm not there to help them, so you've got to do it. You need to live your life for others. That's what we were doing before and that's what you need to be doing now.'"

Carol sat up straight and thought for about five minutes, "Irma, you're right. You're absolutely right. That is what Cheryl would want me to do." There was a light and a purpose in Carol's eyes that had been missing since Cheryl died. It suddenly dawned on Carol, "I'm hungry. No, I'm starving."

It startled Bob and Martha when they heard pans being rattled in the kitchen. They watched in amazement as Carol started scrambling eggs and frying bacon. Martha pitched in joyfully helping Carol fix whatever she wanted.

Irma smiled broadly as she stood in the kitchen doorway. Carol grinned, "Irma, have you eaten?"

The rotund Irma cackled, "Girl, I can always eat." The four of them sat around the kitchen table and ate. Food had never tasted better. It was the first happy meal they had all enjoyed since Cheryl's death.

Before Irma left, she invited the Martins to go to church with her on Sunday. The Martins didn't go to church except on Christmas and Easter. When they went, it was to the largest Episcopalian church in Houston. Carol remembered the church camp she and Cheryl attended the summer they turned twelve. Carol thought of the wonderful feeling she had when she and Cheryl went down front during a service and accepted Jesus as their Lord and Savior. She wanted some more of that feeling of joy.

Bob and Martha hesitated a little at Irma's invitation, but Carol responded right away. "Yes, Irma. I would love to go to church with you." Bob and Martha decided to go also. If nothing else, it was a good family outing they desperately needed.

That Sunday, Irma came by their house so they could follow her. Carol jumped in the car with Irma. Irma laughed at how much change there was in Carol in just a couple of days. She still needed to gain weight, but her skin was a healthy pink and her megawatt smile was back.

Irma's church was a much smaller church than they were used to. When they went inside, they were a little apprehensive to discover they were the only white folks there. If they were uneasy, the black folks sure weren't. They crowded around the Martins, shaking their hands, hugging their necks and making them feel welcome.

After a heartfelt prayer from the pastor to open the service, the choir broke out in song, praising God. The choir and the entire church were swaying with the music and clapping their hands to the beat of the song. Shouts of "Hallelujah!" punctuated the praising of God.

Bob and Carol's eyes were as big around as silver dollars. Carol looked around in wonder thinking, *These people are happy! Honestly and truly happy!* Carol laughed and clapped her hands in delight as she joined in the service worshipping God.

Irma's church was now Carol's church. Carol was there every Sunday morning and every Wednesday night.

One day, Irma, who was a wise woman, asked Carol, "Do you ever hear from Buck?"

Sadness crept over Carol's face. "Not anymore. He tried to call me a few times, but I wouldn't talk to him."

Irma pushed the envelope a bit. "Why not?"

Carol was ashamed. "Irma, I was just awful to him. I blamed him for Cheryl's death and I told him so."

Irma replied, "You do know it was not that boy's fault. The fault lies with the evil men who killed Cheryl."

Carol nodded. "I know that now, but I was so screwed up when Cheryl died. I wasn't thinking straight."

Irma let the subject rest for a while, but later said, "You know I'm a pretty good judge of people. I liked that boy. I thought he was good for you. *And,* I could tell you two loved each other."

Carol sighed, "I still love him. I love him so much it hurts inside, but I know he doesn't love me anymore."

Irma cocked an eyebrow. "How do you know that?"

Carol shook her head. "Irma, I was so mean and hateful to him, I know he couldn't possibly love me now. I'll bet he would be glad if he never saw me again."

Irma replied, "I think you're selling that boy short. I think he's got more sand than that."

THE KENTUCKY DERBY

Buck had a new purpose in life. He was preparing Buttermilk for the Kentucky Derby. Even though he had enough money to pay the entry fee, Buck allowed Ace to pay it like in the past with an understanding of a 50/50 split of winnings. Buck had plenty of money now. He no longer needed Ace's financial backing, but Buck wouldn't make any changes to their business arrangement. As far as Buck was concerned, he and Ace were partners for life.

Buttermilk was training well, at least on the Buttermilk scale. He still only did what he wanted to, when he wanted to, but it seemed that the horse was getting more serious about the workouts. As the historic day in May approached, the excitement and anticipation built in Buck.

When the media found that Buttermilk was entered in the Derby, they smelled a great human interest story, a lightly raced colt with only two races under his belt. Wins in a maiden and an allowance race were hardly the résumé to run a horse in the Kentucky Derby.

Ace was the one who suggested it. "Hey boy, I think you ought to run ol' Buttermilk in the Derby."

Buck was confused. "What derby?"

Ace exclaimed, "What derby? Hell boy, the only derby, the Kentucky Derby!"

Buck sputtered, "Well, it's finally happened. You've gone totally senile. I guess I'm going to have to put you in a home sooner than I thought."

Ace shrugged his shoulders, "If you're scairt, throw up your dress and stay at the house."

The more Buck thought about how ridiculous it was to enter Buttermilk in the Kentucky Derby, the more the idea started to appeal to him. Finally, he announced to Ace, "All right, old man. Let's do it! Let's run Buttermilk in the Kentucky Derby!"

As Buck fist-pumped around the room, Ace rolled his eyes, muttering to himself, "I don't know why that damn kid is so surprised. All my ideas are good."

After Ace paid the huge supplemental fee to enter Buttermilk, the media descended on the ranch like a swarm of locusts. Buck's phone constantly rang. Buck already had 24/7 security for Buttermilk. He now had to have security to keep uninvited people off his property. Buck also had to have his phone number changed.

The questions were all the same. "Why did you enter your horse in the Derby?" "Do you think he has a chance to win?" "How did he get his name?" "What do you like better, horse racing or poker?"

A few reporters got wind of Buck and Ace's relationship and began to call Ace. Ace didn't change his number. He simply told each caller that they could quote him and ranted a string of expletives that would make a sailor blush. It's hard to use a sound bite where every other word is the F-bomb.

When Buck overheard one of Ace's rants, he asked Ace, "Who in the world are you talking to?"

Ace thought for a minute. "I think she said her name was Diane Sawyer with *ABC News*. I don't know. I don't watch the damn news away. I don't need for some talking head to tell me the world's going to hell in a handbasket. I know already know that. Although, if they broadcast what I just told them, word for word, I'd watch that!"

Buck slowly shook his head, "Yeah, well, I wouldn't wait up hoping to see that broadcast. What I heard would have a better chance of making it on a gangsta rap album."

Ace grinned. "That might work. I would make a helluva gangster rapper!" Ace began to flash his version of what a gang sign should look like.

Buck headed for the door. "I'm going to the barn before you decide to bust a cap in my ass." Ace just kept throwing down the Ace Wiggins gang sign, which consisted of his middle finger of each hand thrusting at the ceiling.

Buck, Ace, Ramon and Buttermilk arrived at Churchill Downs three day before the big race. Buck had been to the Kentucky Derby before as a spectator. When he snapped a lead on Buttermilk's halter and led him to his stall, Buck was surprised that he was short of breath because of the spike in his excitement level. Being on the hallowed grounds of the most famous horse race in the world as a fan was one thing, having a horse in the race was totally another. Buck thought, *What the hell is wrong with me? I think I'm hyperventilating. Crap, it's three days before the race. I need to bring it down a notch.*

Churchill Downs was nothing short of spectacular, from its twin spires to the colorful azaleas in different shades of pink and purple. The grounds were manicured, not a blade of grass out of place. The grandstands and private boxes sported the landed gentry. The women tried to outdo each other with flowing sun dresses and broad-brimmed hats, representing every color in the rainbow. The men were tanned from the golf course or tennis court.

One bright yellow sundress brought a sharp pain to Buck's heart. It reminded him of Carol.

The infield was a different world, a mini Mardi Gras with naked breasts, mud wrestling and the occasional passed-out drunk. The infield on Derby day became the party capital of the world.

Something that surprised Buck the most was the top trainers like Dwayne Lucas and Bob Baffert made it a point to look up Buck, shake his hand and wish him luck. Ace remarked about their courtesy. "Those boys are a class act." Buck nodded his head in agreement.

Buck didn't have a problem waking up the Saturday morning of the race because he was still awake from the night before. He was too nervous to sleep. Ace, on the other hand, had no such problem. He slept like a baby. When Ace saw Buck, he said, "Boy, you look like a long-tailed cat in a room full of rockers."

Buck had written out a checklist of everything he needed to do on race day. When he had gone through the list for the tenth time, Ace grinned. "Boy, do we need to hit you with a little elephant tranquilizer?"

In racing, as well as anything else where big money was involved, people look for any edge they can get, legal or illegal. Doping racehorses started as soon as there was the first race. Horses are subject to drug tests, but the criminal chemist is always trying to stay ahead of the testers. Tranquilizers in small doses can act like a stimulant.

Ace said, "I hear they got them a new tranquilizer that's so strong, you gotta dump an ounce of it in the Red River, then haul ass a couple of miles downstream and dip you a bucket of the water. You can shoot your horse up with what's in the bucket!"

Buck teased, "You going to get me some?"

Ace retorted, "Hell no! You do your own damn dirty work." Ace continued, "And don't be buzzing Buttermilk either." A buzzer was a small, battery-operated, electrical device that a jockey could use to give an electrical shock to a horse at a critical part of a race. There has been more than one jockey and trainer suspended from racing for being caught with the illegal buzzer.

Ace knew Buck would never have anything to do with drugs or buzzers, but he enjoyed giving Buck a hard time. The truth was Buck enjoyed it too.

As post time got closer, everyone became more on edge. The air had an electrical charge of anticipation. Buck led a groomed Buttermilk to the saddling paddock. Of course, Buttermilk knew he was about to race, but he was more charged up than usual, prancing around, pulling on the lead. This worried Buck. He didn't want Buttermilk to expend his energy and "wash out" before the race started.

After they tacked Buttermilk, Ramon looked at Buck expectantly. Finally, Buck turned the palms of his hands up. "What do you want from me? The only thing I can tell you is stay on top of him!"

Ramon smiled. "I know, Mr. Buck. I just wanted to hear you say it. It's good luck!"

When all 170,000 people in attendance joined in singing the old Stephen Foster ballad *My Old Kentucky Home,* tears streamed down the cheeks of young and old, alike. It was good to know that some traditions would never change.

The bugler trumpeted the famous "Call to the Post." The hair stood up on the back of Buck's neck. Everyone stopped what they were doing and focused on the racetrack.

The betting favorites were the bright chestnut, American Dreamer, at 3-1, the dappled gray California Kid at 8-1, and the dark bay, Flying Pegasus, who had been bought at auction after the Barker brothers' demise, at 10-1. Bold Buttermilk started at 50-1, but the betting public loves a sentimental story they can get behind. They bet Buttermilk down to 15-1 just before post time. The professional gamblers sneered at such an emotional display for a horse with absolutely no chance to win.

One of the network prognosticators for thoroughbred racing was asked his assessment of Buttermilk's chances. He responded, "Bold Buttermilk has two chances to win, slim and none. And, Slim has caught a train out of town."

There was a short field this year with only nine entries. This year's edition of the Derby was considered one of the toughest in years. Other good horses stayed away, wanting to dodge the formidable duo of American Dreamer and California Kid, both winners of big stakes races.

Buttermilk had drawn the seventh hole, not the best but not the worst either. Buck didn't watch the race from the rail like he did in Buttermilk's first two races. He knew it was stupid, but he felt like that was his and Carol's spot. This time, he and Ace would watch the race from a private box.

The bell rang. The doors flew open. All nine horses bolted down the track to run the mile distance. The loudspeaker blared,

"They're off! American Dreamer broke on top, followed by California Kid and Flying Pegasus." The announcer called off the rest of the horses in their order, finishing with, "Bold Buttermilk in ninth, two lengths behind the field."

The horses flashed by the one-eighth mile marker. At three-eighths, the announcer continued, "It's still American Dreamer by two lengths over California Kid. Flying Pegasus is another half-length back. Bold Buttermilk has moved up and is now seventh."

After the turn, the pack approached the half-mile mark. "At the half-mile, American Dreamer's lead has been cut to one length by California Kid, with Flying Pegasus a neck back in third. Bold Buttermilk has steadily been making up ground since his rocky start. Bold Buttermilk has moved into fourth."

The top four horses distanced themselves from the rest of the field. They made the second turn. "And here they come down the stretch! It's American Dreamer by a neck over California Kid! Flying Pegasus is a head back! But here comes Bold Buttermilk, and he's flying down the track, gaining on the leaders!"

Buck and Ace were on their feet screaming. Buck shouted, "Run, boy, run! Come on, Buttermilk, run!"

Ace was yelling, "Run, you sonofabitch, run! I got money bet on you!"

In Houston there was a Kentucky Derby watch party at the Martin house. As the horses headed down the backstretch, Carol was jumping up and down, screaming, "Run, Buttermilk, run! Come on, boy! You can do it!"

Irma was hollering at the screen, "Run, damn you, run! I got money bet on you!"

With an eighth of a mile left to go, the horses thundered towards the finish line. "It's California Kid by a nose! Now it's

Flying Pegasus, now American Dreamer, now Bold Buttermilk! American Dreamer! Bold Buttermilk! California Kid! Flying Pegasus!"

The horses were lined up in a perfect row, with American Dreamer on the rail, California kid to his right, then Flying Pegasus, and Buttermilk on the outside. Flying Pegasus's jockey drifted him wide in an attempt to bump and impede Buttermilk. Buttermilk eyeballed Flying Pegasus, laid back his ears and tried to bite his antagonist. An intimidated Flying Pegasus swerved away from Buttermilk, ignoring his jockey's urgings.

The four horses streaked across the finish line to the roar of the crowd. "Folks, it's too close to call! It's a photo finish! I don't know who won, but this may be the greatest finish in Kentucky Derby history! What a horse race!"

Ramon was wearing the black and red racing silks for the Buck Morgan Stable. The number on his back for this race was 7. Buck was watching, desperately hoping to see the number 7 displayed on the scoreboard as the winner.

The scoreboard flashed "7." The announcer shouted excitedly, "Bold Buttermilk, considered to be more than just a long shot, is the winner of this year's Kentucky Derby! American Dreamer is second, followed by California Kid in third, and Flying Pegasus finished fourth."

Pandemonium broke out among the spectators. All felt like they had gotten their money's worth at this Derby. The infield bunch was the most raucous. Not only were there numerous barebreasted women, but a dozen naked men celebrated Buttermilk's victory by streaking from one side of the infield to the other.

Buck and Ace snaked their way through the throng of well-wishers. The crowd was pushing towards Buck, wanting to shake his hand or pound him on the back. They got to the winner's circle in time to see the garland of roses placed around Buttermilk's neck.

Each year, a garland of more than four hundred red roses is sewn into a green satin backing with the seal of the Commonwealth on one end, and the Twin Spires and number of the race's current renewal on the other. Each garland is also adorned with a "crown" of roses, green fern and ribbon. The crown, a single rose pointing upward in the center of the garland, symbolizes the struggle and heart necessary to reach the Derby Winner's Circle. The garland was the reason that the Derby was known as "The Run for the Roses."

Buck knew the garland was awesome, but seeing it on Buttermilk brought tears to his eyes. As the picture was taken, Buck thought of how he would have loved to have had Cheryl immortalize it in a painting.

WINS AND LOSSES

Back in Houston, Carol collapsed on the couch in exhaustion from screaming and dancing with joy over Buttermilk's victory. When she saw Buck on TV being interviewed, Carol grabbed a pillow, crushed it to her face and wept loudly.

After Carol had calmed down, Irma took her hand, "Honey, why don't you call that boy? I bet he would be glad to hear from you."

Carol shook her head as she sniffled, "I can't, Irma. Buck winning the Kentucky Derby has made him famous. I wouldn't want him to think that was the reason I wanted to get back together. Besides, you just don't realize how awful I was to him. I'm not sure I could face him."

Irma gave her a hug. "Turn it over to God, baby. If y'all are supposed to be together, God will make it happen." Carol squeezed her hand in gratitude.

Buck was still being congratulated when Ramon tugged on his sleeve. "Mr. Buck, you need to come look at Buttermilk. He's limping pretty bad."

Buck turned to those still wanting to shake his hand,. "Sorry, folks. I appreciate all of your kind words, but something's come up that I have to tend to."

As Buck hurried away, questions were yelled after him. "Are you okay, Buck?" "Is it Buttermilk?" "Is something wrong with Buttermilk?"

When they got to the barn, Buck and Ramon led Buttermilk down the aisle a short distance. The horse was limping on his left front leg. Buck ran his hand down the leg feeling for heat, although he didn't really need to do that. The problem was obvious.

Buck spoke to Ramon and Ace. "I don't need a vet to tell me he's got a bowed tendon."

The Kentucky Derby was the first jewel in the chase for the elusive Triple Crown, which includes the Preakness and the Belmont. All hopes for the Triple Crown were dashed. As much as Buck had some fleeting regrets regarding the Triple Crown, his first concern was Buttermilk's welfare. Buck sent Ramon to get the vet so treatment could begin as soon as possible.

Buck stroked Buttermilk's neck and marveled, "Ace, he didn't bow that tendon walking back to the barn. He bowed it at some point in the race. How in the hell could he run like that on a bowed tendon?"

Ace replied, "Cause the sonofabitch's got heart, that's why!" When the word got out that Buttermilk had won the Kentucky Derby on a bowed tendon, he became a legend. Buttermilk's Kentucky Derby would be mentioned in the same breath as Secretariat's Belmont.

ADALWOLF DITTMAR

A dalwolf Dittmar was a wealthy industrialist. He owned interests ranging from ship building to insurance to banking. His net worth was estimated by *Forbes Magazine* at over 200 billion dollars. Dittmar kept an estate in Louisville that he only visited one week a year, for the Kentucky Derby.

One of the Churchill Downs officials located Buck in the barn. He excitedly whispered in Buck's ear, "Mr. Adalwolf Dittmar wants to speak with you. Can you come to the office?"

Buck shrugged. "Well… okay, I guess."

Buck followed the excited official to the office. When they entered, a tanned, blond man with an expensive haircut and clothes offered his hand. "I wanted to meet you, Mr. Morgan. My name is Adalwolf Dittmar. You have a magnificent horse! Today was even more fun than when I went to Manila for Ali verses Frazier!"

Buck shook his hand. "It's nice to meet you, Mr. Dittmar. I appreciate your kind words."

Dittmar smiled and continued, "We're having a little get-together at my place tonight. I would be honored if you were to attend." When Dittmar smiled, Buck was amazed at how perfect his teeth were.

Buck returned the smile. "Thank you for the invitation. Would I be imposing on you to ask if I could bring my best friend, Wendell Wiggins?"

Dittmar laughed. "You mean Ace Wiggins? That would be outstanding! I love colorful characters like Ace! I will send a car to your hotel at 8 o'clock this evening to pick you gentlemen up."

Buck replied, "That's very generous of you, Mr. Dittmar. I appreciate it."

Dittmar said, "Splendid! And please, my friends call me Wolf." Buck answered, "Great—please call me Buck."

On the way back to the barn to inform Ace of the evening's activities, Buck snickered and thought, *If Dittmar likes colorful, Ace will colorful the shit out of him.*

Buck and Ace were picked up that evening in a stretch-limo that was long and black with darkly tinted windows. The driver was not you normal chauffeur. He was dressed in a black suit, white shirt and black tie. His black shoes had been spit-shined to a mirror finish. His hair was buzz-cut. His eyes were hidden behind black aviator sunglasses.

Despite his attempt at concealment, Buck spotted the bulge of a pistol in a shoulder holster. Key personnel for Dittmar were all carefully screened ex-Navy Seals or ex-Army Rangers. They all carried weapons, but did not need them to kill. They could kill a man silently and quickly with just their hands.

Buck knew Dittmar was wealthy, but all he could do was gawk at the elaborate mansion when he and Ace pulled up in the limo. It had a huge circular fountain with a carved black wolf howling at the moon. Water gushed from the wolf's mouth, replenishing the fountain. The front of the house had four massive stone columns that extended the three stories of the house. It reminded Buck of pictures he had seen of the Taj Mahal.

When a security staff member ushered them in, Buck went into further shock at the sight and sound of a 24-piece orchestra. There were three crystal chandeliers hanging from the ceiling. The floor and the spiral staircase to the upper floors were imported marble. It seemed there was a black-and-white uniformed wait staff stationed every ten yards to attend the needs and whims of the guests.

The partygoers were clothed and coiffed in the latest and most expensive fashion trends. In this group, Rolex watches weren't considered optional but mandatory for a minimum level of survival.

Wolf greeted them. "Gentlemen, how good of you to come! Buck, everyone wants to meet you. Mr. Wiggins, it's a distinct pleasure to meet you. I've heard many wonderful things about you!"

Buck shook Wolf's hand, "Thank you for inviting us. You have a beautiful house, to say the least."

Ace added, "Pretty nice digs for a boat builder."

Wolf erupted in laughter. "Mr. Wiggins, you are living up to your billing! You are as advertised."

Buck thought, *Dittmar, you haven't seen anything yet. Ace has a lot more colorful in him. I hope you can handle it.*

A murmur went through the crowd as the most beautiful woman Buck had ever seen came down the winding staircase from the second floor. Her lustrous, shoulder-length auburn hair framed the face of an angel. Her emerald eyes sparkled with intelligence. Her red lips had just the right amount of pout. Her posture was one of confidence from living a life where she was always in control. The green color of her short party dress exactly matched the shade of her eyes. The neckline of her dress plunged so low that not much of her breasts was left to the imagination. Ace whispered to Buck, "Holy shit!"

The woman embraced Wolf. "Daddy, you've outdone yourself again. This party will be the best one yet."

Wolf turned to Buck. "Precious, I want you to meet Buck Morgan. Buck, this is my daughter Gretchen."

Buck took her hand like it was fragile china, "Ms. Dittmar, it's nice to meet you."

Gretchen's smile revealed the same perfect teeth her father had. "Please, call me Gretchen. You have a magnificent animal! What a race he ran today! I love his name. It's so droll."

Their eyes locked and Buck was mesmerized until he heard Ace mutter, "What am I, chopped liver?"

Buck grinned. "Gretchen, this is Ace. I've heard him described as… colorful."

Gretchen continued smiling as Ace said, "Ma'am, don't pay any attention to what this boy says. Half the time he don't know come here from sic 'em."

Gretchen laughed. "Ace, you are a delight."

Ace raised an eyebrow at Buck. "See there, jackass. I'm a delight." That made Gretchen laugh harder. Wolf, who had been listening, also joined in the laughter. Gretchen grabbed Buck's hand and introduced him to her friends.

Buck liked to have a few beers from time to time, but beer was not on the lubricant menu at this soirée. After his third glass of champagne, Buck was a little dizzy and a little high. Gretchen pushed her body up against his whenever she got the chance. Within an hour of meeting Gretchen, there was very little of her body Buck had not seen, from the gaping of her dress top revealing her breasts to strategically crossing her legs in a manner that gave Buck a view of the tiny, gossamer patch of her camel-toed thong.

Gretchen's lips grazed Buck's ear as she softly said, "Why don't we go up to my room and get better acquainted?" Buck started to get up, but Carol's face flashed in his mind. "Actually, Gretchen, I need to get back. I want to see how Buttermilk is doing."

Gretchen crossed her arms like a petulant child,. "Buck, I'm not used to anyone telling me no."

Buck apologized, "I'm sorry, Gretchen. Some things can't be helped." Before Buck could leave, Gretchen kissed him full on the mouth and slipped her tongue between his lips. Buck momentarily kissed her back before abruptly ending the kiss. "I'm sorry, Gretchen, but like I said, I have to go."

Gretchen batted her gorgeous eyes and flirtatiously said, "Buck, I want you. I want a real man. I'm tired of these pampered and spoiled excuses for men."

Buck laughed nervously. "Gretchen, we just met. I think you may have had a little too much to drink."

Gretchen kissed him on the cheek and winked. "Buck, I know what I want… and I *always* get what I want."

MONACO

The next morning, Buck's cell phone buzzed. "Hi Buck, it's Wolf. Say, a few of us are going to fly to Monaco for a little Kentucky Derby celebration. It would mean a lot to me if you would come. Nothing like having the owner of the horse that won the Derby at a Kentucky Derby party."

Buck couldn't help but chuckle. "Wolf, what was that we were doing last night? I thought *that* was the Kentucky Derby party!"

Wolf laughed. "Last night was just a warm-up. We're just getting started. Listen, I'll take care of everything. I'll send one of my men to pick you up and take you to the airport. We'll hop on my plane for the flight. I've got a place in Monaco where we can stay. I promise you, you will have the time of your life! You've never lived until you've partied in Monaco!"

Buck noticed the invitation didn't include Ace. "Can I bring Ace?"

Wolf hesitated slightly before answering, "Sure… of course… Ace is always welcome."

Buck responded, "Let me check with Ace and I'll call you back."

Wolf replied, "That will be fine. Look forward to hearing from you."

When Buck told Ace about the invitation, Ace snorted, "That's a crock of shit. Why would I want to spend several days with a bunch of rich assholes and listen to their crap? I had enough of that bullshit last night." Ace paused before continuing, "Now, if you want to go, knock yourself out. I'll just stay here and keep tabs on my golden goose."

Ace tried to act like his interest in Buttermilk was strictly financial, but Buck saw Ace stroking Buttermilk's neck and whispering to him whenever Ace thought no one was watching. Buck said, "Well, I might take a run out there to see how the other half lives. It might be pretty interesting."

Ace shrugged, "Whatever, junior."

After calling back Wolf to tell him that it would just be him going on the trip, Buck thought, *I wonder if Gretchen will be on the plane. Half of me doesn't want her there. The other half does want her there, maybe a little too much. I don't know why jumping Gretchen should be such a big deal to me. Carol's out of my life. Hell, I've tried to get back with her. She didn't want it. She hates me! What am I supposed to do? Because of someone who hates me, I'm supposed to keep my hands off what may be the sexiest woman alive?*

Buck's eyes bulged when he saw Wolf's plane. It was a Boeing 757. It had a commercial seating capacity of over two hundred people. The jet's top speed was over 600mph and cruised at 500mph. It could fly a quarter of the way around the world without stopping for fuel.

Dittmar had paid over a hundred million dollars for the plane and spent another fifty million renovating it. It was fitted with twenty Corinthian leather reclining seats, the finest plush carpeting, and was decorated with works of art normally only found in museums. There was a master bedroom at one end of the plane and two smaller bedrooms at the other end. It had a gourmet kitchen equipped to cook any meal desired.

Dittmar employed three pilots, three stewardesses, two maids and a world-class chef as a flight crew. They were paid handsomely and were on call 24 hours a day, 365 days a year. An ex-Seal and an ex-Army Ranger accompanied Dittmar wherever he went. They were rarely more than ten feet away from him unless Dittmar gave explicit orders to the contrary.

When Buck was picked up by the chauffeur/commando, the man in black insisted on carrying his bag to the car. He also carried Buck's bag up the stairs to the plane before handing it off to one of the plane's staff members. Buck thanked him, but got only a curt nod in return. Buck thought, *These special forces types are so uptight, you couldn't drive a 16 penny nail up their asses with a ball-peen hammer.*

The first to greet Buck was Wolf. "Buck, old man, thanks so much for coming! You are going to have a great time!"

Buck responded, "Thanks, Wolf. It was kind of you to invite me."

Gretchen brushed by her father and embraced Buck, giving him a full kiss on the mouth with a hint of a tongue. Wolf roared with laughter, "Buck, I believe you've made yourself a fan!"

Gretchen smiled seductively. "Yes, I am most definitely a fan."

For one of the few times in his life, Buck was speechless. The brazenness of Gretchen in front of her father caused Buck to grin sheepishly. Buck noticed that Wolf wasn't taken aback by Gretchen's behavior. He seemed amused by it.

Gretchen seized Buck's hand. "Come, let me give you a tour of the plane." She showed him the cockpit, kitchen, dining area, theater, lounge, five complete bathrooms, and all three bedrooms. The furnishings and accoutrements were second to none. Buck had to admit he was impressed.

The last room Gretchen showed him was her bedroom. The décor was all white with a large round bed in the center of the room. The mirrored ceiling was especially noteworthy. Gretchen pushed a button and the lights dimmed. Strobe lights began to flash, creating an eerie effect for the room. Gretchen pushed a second button and the bed started to slowly rotate.

Gretchen was dressed in a thin silk dress by Givenchy. It wasn't hard to see that she wore no bra or panties. She grabbed both of Buck's hands and pulled him down on the bed on top of her. She started to kiss him. "Finally, I've got you alone. Buck, I think you're the most exciting man I've ever known." Gretchen kissed him as she rolled her sex against Buck's groin. Buck kissed her back and felt his manhood begin to respond.

Carol's face blazed up in his mind. Buck thought, *Go away! Why are you even here? You don't love me. You hate me. Why do you care who I screw?* Carol's face vanished, but the mood was killed for Buck. Gretchen had managed to wedge her hand down the front of his pants and was playing with her new squeeze toy.

Buck pulled her hand out and shoved himself off her and off the bed. "I'm sorry, Gretchen. This is neither the time nor the place."

An incredulous Gretchen said, "You... have... to... be... kidding... me!" Gretchen pulled her slinky dress off over her head and laid back on the bed in a suggestive pose, "You are turning this down?"

Buck swallowed hard as he surveyed the most perfect body he had ever seen. "It's not you, Gretchen. You are gorgeous. It's me. I have some things I have to sort out."

Gretchen's temper flared as she commanded, "Buck Morgan, you get over here and make love to me…*right now!*"

Buck chuckled. "Gretchen, I don't know who the hell you think you're talking to, but I'm not one of your flunkies. You tell Wolf to land this plane at the next available airport and I will take a commercial flight back to Kentucky."

The naked Gretchen grasped one of Buck's hands and began kissing it as she sobbed, "Buck, I'm sorry. Please don't go. I promise to behave. Please come to Monaco with us!"

Buck's heart softened at the weeping woman. "Okay, Gretchen. I'll come with you, but we do it on my terms, not yours."

Gretchen smiled through her tears,. "Whatever you say, Buck. We'll do it your way."

Buck continued, "Look Gretchen, I'm not saying we can never be together. I'm just saying that for right now, my situation is complicated."

Gretchen slipped back into her dress. "Whatever you say, Buck. Just know that whenever you're ready, I'll be there."

There was a knock on the door. A feminine voice with a French accent said, "*Mademoiselle*, dinner is served." Dinner consisted of ribeyes from Wagyu cattle bred exclusively in Japan. A single ribeye would set you back $2,800 in a pricey restaurant in New York. There was a pineapple salad with the pineapple brand that sold for $15,000 per pineapple. This brand of pineapple was grown in Cornwall, England under thirty tons of manure and soaked in horse urine. The soup was noodles with abalone, Japanese flower mushroom, sea cucumber, dried scallops, chicken, huan ham, pork and ginseng. It was a seven course meal, each course more delicious than the one before.

When he finished, Buck told Wolf, "My compliments to the chef. That was delicious!" At the same time Buck thought, *It was good, but I'd still take a good 'ol chicken-fried steak any day.*

Gretchen watched Buck during dinner. Every time he looked at her, she gave him her biggest smile.

After dinner, Buck and Gretchen sat in two leather chairs in the lounge, sipping cognac. Gretchen smiled. "Buck, I can't wait for you to meet my best friend, Brigitte DuBois. Bridget's father is Pierre DuBois. Pierre is the founder of a huge perfume empire. You'll love Brigitte. She's so much fun! Her parents named her after the old French movie star, Brigitte Bardot. Do you know who Brigitte Bardot was? My Brigitte bears an uncanny resemblance to her namesake."

Buck responded, "If she's the one I'm thinking of—long blonde hair, buxom?"

Gretchen clapped her hands in delight. "Yes, that's the one! My Brigitte has the same blonde hair and big boobs." Gretchen gave a sly smile, "Do you like big boobs, Buck?"

Buck couldn't help but return her smile., "I guess… Really it depends on the girl. With a girl, size is not that big a deal."

Gretchen's smile widened. "A man's size is a big deal to me." Buck actually blushed a little when he remembered Gretchen already knew his size.

When they exited the plane after landing in Monaco, Buck marveled at the security. There, close to one hundred uniformed, private ex-commandos circled around the plane. Buck wondered if even the President of the United States had such tight security.

Wolf, Gretchen, Buck and the rest of the guests loaded into a fleet of black limos. Gretchen managed to sit next to Buck and rested her hand on his thigh as she smiled sweetly. It took over an hour to arrive at their destination. Housing in Monaco was the second most expensive in the world, ranked only behind Hong Kong.

The Dittmar home in Monaco was an immense mansion situated high on a cliff overlooking the Mediterranean Sea. The water glistened in the sunlight. It was the most incredible blue Buck had ever seen. The colorful villas and houses dotting the coastline, completing a picture only found in the finest paintings. The thought of a beautiful painting brought back painful memories of Cheryl. Buck didn't know what was more overwhelming, the lavishness of the mansion or the spectacular view.

After one of the staff showed him to his room and his luggage was delivered, the door burst open and Gretchen bounced in. "Buck, we're going to the Monte Carlo Casino tonight! Brigitte is going to meet us there! You're going to love Brigitte!"

After shooing Gretchen out, Buck laid back on the plush bed. The view from the balcony of his room was breathtaking. Buck thought, *A man could get used to this*. Buck thoughts wandered to Gretchen. *Yes, I get the fact that her clothes are the best money can buy, but does she own anything that doesn't show so much of her tits and ass?*

The Monte Carlo Casino had a VIP private section where your ordinary, run-of-the-mill millionaires weren't allowed. Only the true heavyweights had access to this private section. It had a complete set of multiple gambling tables, six bars and wait staff. Wolf had reserved the entire VIP section.

The fleet of limos deposited Wolf and his guests at a heavily guarded private entrance to the casino. The casino made sure that its billionaire clients did not have to rub elbows with the millionaire riff-raff. As they made their entrance, Gretchen had intertwined her arm with Buck's. She pulled free and squealed, "Brigitte!"

A voice called out, "Gretchen!"

The two women ran together, embraced and kissed. The kiss was not your usual peck on the cheek that is reserved for best friends. It was full on the lips. It caused Buck to raise an eyebrow, but he noticed no one else paid any attention to it.

The women held hands as Gretchen pulled Brigitte over to meet Buck. "Brigitte, this is Buck!" Buck extended his hand for the handshake he expected. Brigitte ignored Buck's hand, wrapped her arms around him, pressed her body to his and kissed him on the mouth.

Gretchen giggled, "See Buck, I told you that you would like her!"

Brigitte whispered in Buck's ear, "Gretchen has told me *all* about you." Buck was already on his heels, but Brigitte's French accent set him back even farther.

Brigitte DuBois was indeed the spitting image of Brigitte Bardot. She had long blonde hair and a full figure. Gretchen had the classic fashion model body. Brigitte's body was more the earth mother type. Buck couldn't help but notice that Brigitte and Gretchen must have shopped at the same stores as both their dresses did not leave much to the imagination.

Standing side by side, anyone could have made a case that Gretchen and Brigitte were the most glamorous women on the face of the Earth.

Wolf approached Buck with what looked like a velvet box. He thrust it into Buck's hands. "Buck, old man, I am giving all my guests $50,000 in chips. Good luck at the tables!" As Wolf wheeled around to visit his other guests, a member of the casino staff followed him, pushing a cart stacked with the velvet boxes.

A stunned Buck looked at Gretchen. "I can't take this… This is too much."

Gretchen kissed him on the cheek. "Of course you can, darling. Money means nothing to Daddy. Now, let's go play blackjack." Gretchen and Brigitte each grabbed an arm and steered Buck to the closest blackjack table.

Buck sat between the girls. All three played, but Buck was the only one who stayed money ahead. Gretchen and Brigitte bet recklessly as if the chips held no value. Buck realized that neither one of them knew the value of a dollar. It was Monopoly money to them.

As they played their hands, Brigitte laid her hand high on Buck's thigh. As she gently squeezed his leg, Buck cut his eyes over to Gretchen to see if she was aware that her so-called best friend was making a play for him. Gretchen was watching. She smiled as she moved her hand across Buck's lap to Brigitte's hand. Buck was certain he was about to witness a cat-fight with Gretchen jerking Brigitte's hand off his leg.

Buck's eyes went wide in disbelief when Gretchen patted Brigitte's hand and started to squeeze it. Buck thought, *What in the holy hell have I gotten myself into? I've never seen women act like this.* Then Buck suddenly remembered Donna and Rhonda from the country bar. *Well, maybe I have. Now, I have to decide what I'm going to do.*

The rest of the night was relatively uneventful, if one can consider a night at the Monte Carlo Casino uneventful. The party lasted until 5:00am before they boarded the limos and convoyed back to the Dittmar mansion.

Once inside, Wolf motioned Buck over to the sitting area. Gretchen and Brigitte walked arm in arm until they disappeared from view. Wolf gestured to a leather chair. "Sit down, my boy. I've got something I want to discuss with you."

As Buck took a seat, a staff member approached with a tray of drinks. Buck declined, "No thanks. I've had enough for one night."

Wolf selected a glass and began to sip,. "Buck, my little girl has taken quite a shine to you."

Buck replied, "I like Gretchen. She's certainly a beautiful woman."

Wolf beamed proudly, "Yes she is. Since her mother was killed in a plane crash, Gretchen has been my whole life. I'm afraid I've spoiled her a bit. I just can't deny her whatever she wants." Wolf paused as he swirled his drink. "Let me get to the point. I like you. I think you're your own man and you know what you're doing. I want to back you, Buck."

Buck was a little confused. "Back me how, Wolf?"

Wolf slapped his knee. "In anything you want to do. I have unlimited resources. I will supply any amount of money you need. We will be partners, but I will be a silent partner. You will be completely in charge."

Buck continued to question him,. "Why would you do that?"

Wolf responded, "Buck, I've gotten wealthy by making smart investments, but I don't invest in things. I invest in people. I invest in winners. I know a winner when I see one, and Buck, you are a winner!"

Buck said, "Wolf, that's a very generous offer. I will definitely give it some thought."

Wolf exclaimed, "Splendid! You just say the word and my people will make it happen!"

Buck shook Wolf's hand. "Thanks for everything, Wolf, but I'm bushed. I'm going to turn in. Good night."

Wolf replied, "Sleep well, my friend."

When Buck opened his bedroom door, what he saw made him whisper, "What the hell?" Gretchen and Brigitte were seated on his bed. The sheet covered their lower bodies, but they were naked from the waist up. Gretchen laughed softly as she patted the bed between her and Brigitte, "Come join us, Buck. We want to show you some things that you've never seen before."

Buck's mind whirled as he quickly calculated his decision, two drop-dead gorgeous women waiting to have sex with him against the memory of an old girlfriend who hated him. It was a no-brainer. Buck began to remove his clothes as the girls devoured him with their eyes.

When Buck was naked, Gretchen pulled back the sheet revealing that she and Brigitte were as naked as the day they were born. Buck laid down between them as the girls snuggled up to him, one on each side. He had an arm around each girl as he alternated kissing each. Gretchen and Brigitte were exploring his body with their hands. Buck felt his desire rise.

Out of nowhere, Carol's face appeared in a vision before him. Buck groaned, *I just don't get it, Carol. Why are you haunting me? You're the one who broke it off between us!* As Buck to tried refocus on the two women, he groaned louder, "Dammit, Carol. Leave me alone!"

Gretchen was startled as she looked up. "Who's Carol?"

Brigitte stopped what she was doing. "Yes, who is Carol?"

Buck started to cuss as he shoved himself off the bed and began to dress. "Dammit all to hell! I don't believe this shit!"

Gretchen jumped from the bed and tried to pull him back. "Buck, what's wrong? Please come back to bed. If we did something wrong, I promise we'll do better!"

After Buck had pulled his boots back on, he looked at the bewildered girls. "Look, it's nothing y'all did. Honestly, it has nothing to do with you. I'm just going through some things. It's… it's… hell, it's just too complicated to get into." Buck left the bedroom and spent the night sleeping on one of the couches in the sitting area. One of the staff members spread a blanket over him as he slept.

The next morning when Buck woke up, the first thing he saw was Wolf sitting in a chair watching him sleep. As Buck sat up, yawned and stretched, Wolf said, "Good morning, Buck. I wish you had slept in your bed. That couch couldn't have been that comfortable."

Buck rubbed the sleep from his eyes. "Actually, it wasn't that bad. I slept pretty well, all things considered."

Wolf got to the point. "Gretchen spent the night in my room crying her eyes out. What happened between you and her last night? She genuinely doesn't seem to know."

Buck became very serious. "First, let me apologize to her and to you. The last thing I wanted to do was to hurt her feelings. The thing is, Gretchen and I are just not a good fit. I also want you to know I tried not to do anything to lead her on. I just couldn't seem to discourage her."

Wolf smiled. "Yes I know. My daughter is very headstrong. When she decides she wants something, she goes after it until she gets it." After a brief pause, Wolf continued, "Is there anything I can do to make things better between you and her?"

Buck shook his head. "I'm sorry but no. Also, I'm going to have to turn down your gracious offer to become my partner. I have a partner and I don't ever foresee a situation where I'd replace him. If you will have one of your people call me a cab, I want to catch a flight back to Kentucky."

Wolf retorted, "Nonsense! I'll have my plane fly you back. Just let me know when you're ready to leave."

Buck replied, "Wolf, I don't want to put you out. What if you need to use your plane?"

Wolf smiled, "Buck, I have more than one plane."

When Buck left the Dittmar mansion, he shook Wolf's hand, but Gretchen was nowhere to be seen. Buck had only been gone for two days, but when the plane touched down on U.S. soil, relief flooded through Buck as if he had been away for years.

THE CLEAN BREAK

Buck headed to the barn to see Ace, Ramon and Buttermilk. Ace saw him coming down the barn aisle carrying his luggage. "Well, look who's here. If it isn't Mr. Hot Shit himself." As Buck shook his hand, Ace added, "Well boy, did you find out how the other half lives?"

Buck replied, "I damn sure did. It was interesting, but I wouldn't want to live there."

Ace asked, "And why wouldn't you want to live in a place with hot women and plenty of money?"

Buck chuckled, "Well for one thing, their food is a little peculiar. We had a pineapple salad that was really good, but…"

Ace snapped, "But, what?"

Buck grinned, "This pineapple was grown under a manure pile and washed in horse piss."

Ace exploded, "Boy, I'll slap you sillier than you already are. I was born at night, but I wasn't born last night! Don't be trying to stack a bunch of shit on me!"

Buck put up his hands as he laughed, "Believe what you want to believe. I'm just telling you what I was told. And there's one other thing. There was no chicken-fried steak."

Ace was now shouting at the top of his lungs, "No chicken-fried steak! No chicken-fried steak! That tears a new one! What kind of bunch of damn heathens are over there! A man can't live without chicken-fried steak!"

Buck hugged Ramon in greeting and spent several hours in the stall with Buttermilk. He hadn't realized how much he had missed the horse. And he wasn't for sure, but it seemed like Buttermilk may have missed him too.

At first, celebrity is a rush. Everyone applauding and praising is a huge boost to one's ego. The new had already started to wear off for Buck. "Ace, as soon as the doc says Buttermilk can travel, let's pack up and head back to Texas."

Ace grumbled, "It's about damn time. I was wondering when you were going to get tired of playing Mr. Hot Shit!"

A week after they got back to Texas, the phone rang. It was Gretchen. "Hi Buck, how are you?"

Buck responded unenthusiastically, "I'm fine, Gretchen. How are you?"

Gretchen's voice caught. "Uh… to tell you the truth, I've been better. I miss you Buck. I called to just hear the sound of your voice."

Buck was at a loss for words before saying, "Gretchen, I appreciate your call, but I don't think this is a good idea."

Gretchen wailed, "I just don't understand. I love you. Why don't you love me?"

Buck replied, "Gretchen, it's just not that simple."

As Gretchen sobbed, Buck briefly gave some consideration to telling her that he was in love with another woman. He discarded that idea when he remembered what happened with the Barker brothers. He didn't know that the Dittmars would be that brutal and vindictive, but Buck knew that Wolf had more money than the Mob. He decided not to take any chances.

Finally, Gretchen spoke again. "Well, can we at least be friends?"

Buck said, "I know this is hard. I never wanted to hurt you. Maybe one day we can be friends, but right now is not the time. When and if the timing is ever right, I will call you. I'm sorry Gretchen, but that's the best I can do. Goodbye, Gretchen."

Gretchen sniffed, "Goodbye, Buck."

Buck felt like a heel hurting her like that, but he knew that a clean break meant less pain to her over the long run.

HORSE TRADING

Two weeks after they got back to Texas, Buck received a call from security at his front gate. "Mr. Morgan, there is a Mr. Wolf Dittmar here to see you. Should I let him in?"

Buck hesitated slightly, "Okay... sure... let him in."

When the big black limo pulled up, Buck was waiting on the front porch. Wolf got out and bounded up the steps, shaking Buck's hand. "How are you, old man? It's good to see you."

Buck smiled, "I've been fine, Wolf. How are things?"

Two of Buck's security detail had followed the car up the drive. When Wolf's bodyguards saw them, they quickly exited, standing between them and their boss. They were like dogs staring each other down in a pissing contest.

When Wolf noticed the confrontation, he commanded, "Stand down, men. Get back in the car."

Buck added, "You two go back to the gate. This man is my friend."

Buck turned to Wolf. "Come in out of this sun. The only thing I have to offer you is iced tea." After his drunken trip to Monaco, Buck decided he didn't care as much for alcohol and the effect it had on him. He didn't even keep beer in the fridge anymore—a fact Ace constantly bitched about.

Wolf said, "Actually, iced tea sounds pretty good."

After Buck retrieved the ice tea, they sat in the living room. Buck asked, "What brings you to my neck of the woods?" Buck was hoping against hope it wasn't Gretchen.

Wolf sipped on his tea. "I know you weren't interested in my last business proposal, but I have another offer I'd like to make you. I want to buy Buttermilk. I have a cashier's check in my briefcase made out to you for $50,000,000."

Buck was in mid-swallow of his tea. He choked, then coughed it up. When Buck finally got his breath, he declared, "Wolf, I'm sorry, but that's the craziest thing I've ever heard! The max you could possibly win at the track over the balance of his racing career would be $15,000,000, tops! You know he's gelded so race purses are it. You would be guaranteed to lose at least $35,000,000."

Wolf nodded his head in agreement. "Believe me, old man, I know the numbers. I still want to buy your horse."

Buck shrugged in amazement. "I don't know what to say. I have to talk to Ace. When I have an answer, I'll call you. If I sold him to you, what would you do with him?"

Wolf smiled. "I'd race him, of course. He's a racehorse. I would also hire the best trainer in the world."

Buck was curious. "Who would you hire?"

Wolf laughed. "I'd hire you. I will pay you $5,000,000 a year to train him. I will buy or build a state-of-the-art training facility. If you want to add more horses, we will."

Wolf pulled out the check and laid it on the table. "I'm going to leave this here. If we have a deal, deposit it in your bank."

After Wolf left, Buck called Ace, "Get your old ass over here! You're not going to believe this shit!"

Ace whistled when he read the check. "Boy, this will buy a mess of chicken and dumplings. What are you gonna do?"

Buck replied, "Well, I've been thinking on that. I'm not going to do it for two reasons. One, you're my partner and it wouldn't be right to replace you for money."

Ace interrupted, "Are you nuts? If I was offered that kind of money to replace you, I would change you out like a dirty shirt!"

Buck just laughed, "Sometimes, old man, you are full of more shit than a Christmas turkey. You would do no such thing."

Ace ducked his head. "Well, maybe not. You ain't much, but you're all I got. Alright, you said two reasons. What's the second?"

Buck responded, "The second reason is because I wouldn't be working for Wolf."

Ace was confused. "I don't get it. Who would you be working for?"

Buck answered, "Gretchen."

Ace disagreed. "I don't think that makes any sense. Why do you think she would be calling the shots?"

Buck raised his eyebrows. "Think about it, Ace. If it was Wolf wanting to get into racing, why would he buy a gelding? That's just too short-term a deal for that kind of money. I'm telling you, it's Gretchen."

Ace thought it over. "Well, maybe you're right."

Buck replied, "I'm right!"

Ace continued, "You have a chance to probably marry one of the hottest women in the world. Plus, be a part of a family who can't even count all their damn money. Talk about hitting the daily double! And you turn up your nose at it."

Buck said, "I know I'm certifiable, but as crazy as it might seem, it would be like a death sentence to me. I would no longer be me."

Ace looked at Buck. "It's Carol, isn't it?"

Buck responded, "Shut up. I don't want to talk about it."

JULIE STRONG

J ulie Strong was a professional poker player, but she wasn't an ordinary player. There wasn't anything ordinary about Julie.

Her grandparents were on the last helicopter leaving Saigon before it fell into North Vietnamese hands in 1975. They settled in Los Angeles in the Vietnamese community. They made their living the same way they did in the old country: they were merchants at the daily bazaar.

When the Nguyens gave birth to Huong, it was the happiest day of their lives since leaving Viet Nam. They stressed education to the daughter on a daily basis. The Nguyens were determined Huong was going to lead a better life than theirs.

Huong graduated high school at the top of her class and was offered a full scholarship at Stanford University. She graduated with honors as a CPA. Huong met Jackson Strong, a Harvard-educated attorney, at a political fundraiser. They fell in love and were married.

Huong and Jack were career orientated, but finally decided to have one child, Julie. Julie was born into wealth and privilege, attending the finest private schools. When it was time for college, Julie maxed out every admissions criteria. She was offered a scholarship at Cal Tech, arguably the most difficult university in the country to gain admittance.

Jack responded to the offer by declining it, telling admissions that they didn't need the financial assistance. He suggested they use Julie's scholarship for another deserving party. Julie enrolled at Cal Tech using her family's money for tuition and books. Jack also bought a townhouse for Julie in a gated community, close to the Cal Tech campus.

Julie eventually graduated with a PhD in nuclear physics. Then her life took a drastic turn. She took a week's vacation to Las Vegas to mull over her many job offers. One night she stepped into the casino at the Bellagio. Julie knew the basics of poker, but had never actually played the game.

She was shocked at how easy it was for her to beat the other players. Her superior intellect could process the possible hands of her competitors in seconds. Julie found she could also read the facial expressions of the other players, even the most stoic.

Julie went back to her room that night a $25,000 winner. She lay in bed, giggling. None of her academic accomplishments ever provided the thrill that Texas Hold 'Em did. At the end of the week, Julie returned to Pasadena, wondering how she was going to tell her parents that she was forsaking a guaranteed career as a nuclear physicist to play cards.

Her parents went nuclear, raging, threatening and finally pleading. Julie settled it, saying, "Look Mom, Dad, if I flop as a poker player, my degree isn't going anywhere. I can always fall back on it." Jack and Huong still did not like it, but agreed that maybe it was for the best to try something else before establishing her career.

The first time the Strongs saw their daughter on a televised tournament, they were dismayed. A lot of oriental women are slight on top. Julie was well-endowed and showed it with a plunging neckline. They immediately called Julie demanding an explanation.

Julie responded, "Dad, in spite of the gains that have been made, our society is still sexist. In our male dominated culture, men have no qualms about taking advantage of the good 'ol boy network. I'm just doing the same thing, in reverse. Every time a male player glances at my cleavage, he is distracted from his game. Turnabout is fair play."

Jack still didn't like it, but Huong said, "Now that I understand the reason, I think it's a good strategy." Huong continued, laughing, "In fact, the cost of push-up bras in your case may be tax deductible."

Julie had more going on in the looks department besides big breasts. Her shoulder-length, soft black hair framed an exquisite face highlighted by almond-shaped black eyes, high cheek bones, arching black eyebrows and full lips that caused men's hearts to race. Most men were torn between her face and her cleavage.

Buck first met Julie Strong when she showed up at the weekly poker game at the Hyatt. Ace had invited her. At the same time, he warned Buck, "You better have your head out of your ass, playing against her. The girl is as good a card player as I've seen, including you, Mr. Hot Shit. And if you start gawking and drooling like most the idiots who play against her, she's gonna end up with your money, your ranch and Buttermilk."

Buck smirked, "Who the hell you think you're talking to? I can handle her."

Ace replied, "Whatever you say, Cider Boy."

Even though Buck had seen Julie several times on television, he was not prepared for her stunning physical presence until he met her in person. Julie extended her hand. "Hi, I'm Julie Strong. You must be Buck. I'm a big fan of yours at the card table and the race track."

Buck stammered, "Uh… yeah… I'm Buck. It's nice to meet you, and I am also a big fan of yours." Behind her back, Ace was pointing at his own ear, reminding Buck that he was getting cider in his ear.

The poker game was a blur to Buck. Luck was the only thing that kept him from getting wiped out, calling when he should have folded, folding when he should have raised. Buck simply hit long shots where he shouldn't have even been in the pot. Several times Julie raised an eyebrow at his luck. All Buck could do was grin, sheepishly.

The rest of the players weren't so fortunate. Ace called the game at sun-up with Julie being over $200,000 ahead. After everyone else had left, including Ace, Buck ordered breakfast from room service for Julie and him.

As they ate, Julie remarked, "You play an interesting game, Buck. I could never figure out what you were going to do next."

Buck laughed, almost spitting out a mouthful of eggs. "Hell, I'm not surprised. How could you tell what I was going to do when I didn't know myself? You totally screwed me up. I just hope you know that I'm a better player that what I showed tonight!"

Julie smiled. "Really, Buck? And just how did I screw you up?"

Buck good-naturedly responded, "The dumb act won't wash, Miss Nuclear Physicist. You know exactly your power over men and you certainly know how to use it. I'm Exhibit A."

Julie replied in an exaggerated southern accent, "Why, Mr. Morgan, I declare I don't know what you mean. You are about to give me the vapors." Buck and Julie both laughed hysterically.

As they wiped tears from their eyes, Buck said, "Now don't get me wrong, I'm not saying you get by on just your looks. Ace told me you were as good a player as he's ever seen. And Ace throws around compliments like they were manhole covers. After watching you play first hand, I agree with him."

When breakfast was over, they talked for another two hours about their past. At one point, Buck thought, *Maybe I can finally get over Carol with this girl. Could I love her like I love Carol? I don't know… maybe.*

It was time to get some sleep as they were exhausted. Before they separated, Buck made a date with Julie for dinner that night. They gave each other a light hug and Buck gave Julie a peck on the cheek. When his lips touched her cheek, sparks flew. Both were startled and laughed it off. Buck wondered, static electricity? Or something else?

That night over a candlelit dinner in a private room at a famous steak house, they shared their hopes and dreams, sincerely and honestly. When Buck told her about Carol and Cheryl, Julie covered his hand with hers, caressing it gently. "Oh Buck, how hard that must have been for you."

Buck replied, "It was the worse time in my life, but I know that life goes on."

Julie nodded her head in agreement, "It sounds like you did everything you could have done."

Buck did hold back a few things about his life. He did not tell Julie about killing the Barker brothers. He didn't know if that was something he'd ever share with anyone else.

After dinner, Buck drove Julie back to the Hyatt. He parked his pickup and escorted her into the lobby. As he gave her another peck on the cheek goodnight, Julie smiled as she asked, "Do you want to come up to my room?"

Buck hesitated, "Are you sure that's what you want? There's still lots of bad stuff about me you don't know."

Julie hugged him tightly and whispered in his ear, "Buck, I'm a grown woman. I can take care of myself."

Julie only had two other sexual experiences in her life, both in college. One fling was with a dashing anthropologist who fancied himself the next Indiana Jones. Julie did too until she got to know him better. The second was a grad school professor whom she admired deeply for his work in nuclear physics. When Julie realized she was just one in a string of worshipping female students, she ended their relationship.

Once in her room, Buck and Julie embraced passionately. They surprised each other with their urgency at tearing off each other's clothes. Buck admired Julie's body. Its physical beauty was the equal of Gretchen.

During their lovemaking, Buck was able to get completely lost in Julie. Afterwards, Julie snuggled up to him and whispered, "That was wonderful. Now I know what all the fuss about sex is about."

Buck gently kissed her on the lips. "That was pretty awesome for me too."

Buck and Julie became inseparable. Either she was in Texas or he was in California. Their time together was filled with laughter and happiness. They went to poker tournaments together, but only one of them would enter while the other coached from the rail. They never wanted to play against each other again.

Ace was even happy about his choice in women. "I like that girl. She's got her head on straight. Besides, when your luck finally runs out, she can make a living for both of you playing cards."

Buck protested, "I'll have you know, old man, I'm just as good at Hold 'Em as she is, maybe better."

Ace snorted, "Don't try to bullshit a bullshitter."

Buck did wonder who was better, him or Julie. If he was honest, he might have to admit it was her.

CELEBRITIES

T elevision made national celebrities of Buck and Julie. The public couldn't get enough of the Kentucky Derby winner/poker player and his gorgeous girlfriend and colleague on the professional poker circuit. Everyone wanted to know all about their version of the lifestyle of the rich and famous. They were hounded wherever they went by the media. Buck began to wonder if he could somehow justify shooting the paparazzi.

Carol had to change the channel whenever something came on about Buck and Julie. It thrilled her to see Buck, but tore her heart out to see him with Julie. Many nights Carol cried herself to sleep. *I have messed up my life, but even though it's not with me, I'm glad Buck's happy. He deserves it after what I did to him.*

Buck and Julie were invited to all the A-list parties from coast to coast. Halfway during the first party, Buck turned to Julie. "Are you having fun?"

Julie knew what he meant. "Not really."

Buck said, "Good, let's blow this popsicle stand. These pretentious assholes are driving me crazy."

Julie giggled. "If you're waiting on me, you're walking backward!" From then on, they respectfully declined all invitations.

Yet, something was wrong. Both of them felt it.

One night Julie sat up her bed. "Buck, I love you. I love you like I've never loved another man, but something is missing."

An alarmed Buck replied, "Julie, what could be wrong? We were made for each other!"

Julie responded, "It has just been a feeling, but now I know what it is."

Buck dreaded the answer as he asked, "What?"

Tears streamed down Julie's face. "It's Carol. I don't think you've ever gotten over her. As much as I love you, I can't live my life with her looking over my shoulder!"

Buck denied it. "Julie, that's just crazy. It's over between Carol and me. She hates me. I can't love someone who hates me."

Julie wiped away tears as she sniffled, "I would love to believe that, but I don't… I want you to look me in the eyes and make me believe that you don't love her."

Buck emphatically said, "That will be easy! I don't… I don't…" Buck's eyes dropped as he could no longer look return Julie's gaze.

Buck thought, *What the hell is wrong with me? Julie is great. She got looks and intelligence. I must be a total idiot.* Julie softly sobbed, "Buck, I want you to leave. When you get your head straight and can tell me you no longer love Carol, I'll be waiting for you."

A despondent and dejected Buck called a taxi to take him to the airport to catch a flight back to Texas. He never went back in the bedroom to say goodbye to the crying Julie. Buck felt it would make it worse for her.

When he told Ace what had happened, Ace patted his shoulder. "That's a tough one."

Buck raised his eyebrows. "What, no smart ass remarks?"

Ace shrugged. "I reckon you been kicked enough for one day."

THE CALLING

Buck was slowly being enveloped by a black cloud of depression. He started drinking more than he should to try to dull the pain. Buck reached the end of his rope. He would have to high jump to reach the bottom of a snake's belly.

One morning when he was in the barn and he thought no one else was around, Buck dropped to his knees. "God, I don't know if You're out there. I don't even know if You're real. If You are really there, I need some help! I have to have some help from somewhere. God, please help me."

Ramon had heard Buck's desperate prayer from the tack room. Ramon stepped through the door. "Mr. Buck, you have done a good thing. God is real and He will help you."

Buck gave Ramon a hug and gratefully smiled, "Thanks, Ramon. You are a true friend. I hope you're right about God being real."

Ramon grinned. "Oh, He is real, Mr. Buck. I talk to Him every day."

At 6 o'clock the next Sunday morning, Buck was awakened by a voice. "Get up." Buck bolted upright in his bed. His first thought was one of the old Barker gang had come to extract revenge. Buck grabbed his .38 off his nightstand, but he couldn't see anyone. He carefully searched the rest of his house. The search yielded nothing.

Buck was still a little unnerved, so he laid the gun by his pillow and closed his eyes to try to get back to sleep. The voice said again. "Get up."

Buck sprang out of bed brandishing his pistol, "Where are you?" He was met by silence.

Buck knew he had not imagined the voice. "Who are you?"

The voice said, "I am."

Buck realized the voice was in his head. Buck was already on edge, but the realization that the voice was in his head totally spooked him. With his own voice trembling, Buck asked again, "Who are you?"

The mysterious voice answered again, "I am."

Buck was shocked to his core when he recalled that his daddy, while preaching his false religion, referred to the God of Abraham as "The Great I Am." Buck fell to his knees. He couldn't believe that he was actually having a conversation with God himself. Buck inquired, "Sir, what do you want from me?"

God said, "Trinity Fellowship in Decatur. I want you there this morning."

Buck knew nothing about Trinity Fellowship in Decatur. It was a satellite campus for Trinity Fellowship in Amarillo. The local campus pastor was Frankie Garcia. Frankie was a godly man who, with his wife Tonya, had led a miraculous revival of the local church.

Buck had never been to church before, having been turned off as a child with the hypocrisy of his daddy. Obadiah and Ruth never took him to church as a child. They didn't go because Obadiah said the preachers in churches didn't know enough about the Bible to teach him anything. He knew much more than they did.

Buck sat in the back row. He became amazed as his heart was stirred and touched by the music from the praise team and the message of God's forgiveness delivered by video from Jimmy Evans.

At the end of the service, Frankie and Tonya stood at the bottom of the stage. Frankie said, "If there's anyone here who does not know Jesus Christ as his Savior, please come down and meet Him." Buck began to cry as he slowly walked to the alter.

Frankie grasped Buck's hands. "Hi son, I'm Frankie. Would you like to meet Jesus?"

Buck whispered to Frankie, "Would you think I was crazy if I told you that God spoke to me today and told me to come here?"

Frankie smiled as he shook his head. "No, son. I wouldn't call you crazy. I would call you blessed."

Buck confessed, "Frankie, I've killed men and caused pain and misery to the one person I love the most in this world. Do you think God will forgive all that?"

Frankie's smile widened. "Son, our God is a big God. The Bible promises us that *all* our sins can be forgiven, no matter how big they are." Buck sighed in relief.

Frankie continued, "Jesus is the Son of God. He was sent to this earth to sacrifice Himself for the forgiveness of our sins so that we may spend eternity in Heaven. Do you believe that, son?"

Frankie's words resonated in Buck's spirit. He knew Frankie was speaking the truth. Buck replied in a clear voice, "Yes sir, I do!"

Frankie laughed joyously, "Because of you expression of faith, God is faithful to forgive your sins. You will spend eternity with Him!" Both men embraced with tears streaming down their faces.

FIGHT FOR HER

O n the drive back to the ranch from church, Buck experience a peace that passed all understanding. There was now only one thing that was still a source of pain for Buck, his memory and longing for Carol. There was a hole in his heart where she belonged. As he thought about Carol, a still, small voice in his mind said, "Fight for her." Buck thought, *She hates me. She won't even see me. How do I fight for her?* The voice said again, "Fight for her." Buck came to a decision. He was going to fight for Carol. That night, Buck packed a suitcase, loaded it in his pickup and headed south to Houston.

The next morning, Buck was the first one in line when the doors opened to the massive lobby of Houston National Bank. Buck approached the information desk. "I would like to see Carol Martin."

The receptionist asked, "Is she expecting you?"

Buck replied, "No ma'am, she's not."

The receptionist gave him a stern look,. "Does Ms. Martin know what this is in reference to?"

Buck insisted, "Look ma'am, this is personal. Just tell her that Buck Morgan is here to see her. If she doesn't want to see me, I'll leave quietly."

The receptionist softened. "Say, aren't you the owner of that horse that just won the Kentucky Derby? I'm a big racing fan!"

Buck laughed, "Yes ma'am, I am."

The receptionist dialed her phone and said, "Ms. Martin, there's a Buck Morgan here to see you." Her face fell. She looked at Buck sorrowfully. "I'm sorry, Mr. Morgan. She hung up."

Buck started for the exit, resigned to his fate.

"Buck! Buck!"

Buck spun around to see Carol running across the lobby floor in high heels, calling his name. Buck ran to meet her.

Carol jumped into Buck's arms, sobbing and kissing him. Tears unashamedly ran down Buck's face as he swung her around. Carol blubbered, "Honey, I have missed you so. I was afraid I had messed things up to the point that you wouldn't want me back. And when Buttermilk won the Kentucky Derby, I didn't want you to think it was the reason I wanted you back."

Buck replied, "Baby, take how much you've missed me and multiply it by a thousand. That's how much I've missed you. I have an important question to ask you: will you marry me?"

Carol shouted, "Will I marry you? Of course, I will marry you! Yes! Yes! A thousand times, yes!"

At that point several hundred people, in various lines to do business with the bank, began to applaud. Soon everyone in the lobby was clapping as loudly as they could. The receptionist and the women tellers who knew Carol were all crying and borrowing Kleenex from each other.

An embarrassed Carol grabbed Buck's hand to lead him to the elevator, then down the hall to her office. Carol told her secretary, "I don't want to be disturbed, please!" She pulled Buck into her office and locked the door.

Acknowledgements

I am grateful for the constant support of my wife, Tina, and my children: Jacob, Caleb, and Sarah.

Thank you to Missy Brewer for editing this book, to Michael Campbell for the book design, and to Bryan Gehrke for the cover design.

You can email me at williamjoinerauthor@gmail.com.

Learn more at
www.williamjoinerauthor.com

Joining the Rewards Club on my website is 100% FREE and scores you a FREE eBook copy of *American Entrepreneur*. As a Rewards Club member you will receive monthly notices of future give-a-ways and special promotions. My pledge to you is you won't receive an email from me more than once a month.

www.williamjoinerauthor.com

Printed in Great Britain
by Amazon